lust and lollipops

SURVIVAL OF THE MATED

LOLA GLASS

To all of the broccoli sacrificed in the making of this book
I still wish you were chocolate

one

MOLLY

I COLLAPSED on the couch and stared up at the ceiling for a good long minute. Everything was packed, and there was no longer any reason to delay the inevitable. I'd said goodbye to everyone at work the day before, and hugged my grandma tightly after she fed me dinner that night.

It was barely six in the morning, but in a few minutes, I'd be in an armored vehicle.

And on my way to the *Fae Bachelorette* mansion.

Fae, as in magical beings. Some of them could change into animals, while others had dangerous mental magic.

They had come out of hiding and saved the day when us humans nearly ended the world with nuclear warfare a few years earlier. Afterward, they offered their price for letting us return to normal life:

Mates.

As in, wives.

And husbands.

But mostly wives.

Most fae were men, thanks to their screwy genetics.

Said screwy genetics required them to take mates in order to become immortal, so all of them wanted someone to hook up with.

After the war ended, every human under twenty-five had their blood tested. Most people received a clean bill of health, saying that the fae required nothing from them.

But some of us didn't.

And I was one of those.

Their ridiculous *Fae Bachelorette* TV show had begun airing immediately. They gave the compatible human women a month to choose between a dozen fae guys. Most humans had become obsessed with watching it ever since.

Myself not included.

Knowing I was going to be forced to participate in the show at some point put a real damper on the drama's excitement for me.

Bachelorette had been running constantly in the four years since, with just a few days between each new season that started.

Considering I'd turned twenty-four a few months earlier, and was on the oldest end of the compatibility spectrum, I'd known my days of freedom were numbered. For whatever reason, compatibility faded around a person's twenty-fifth birthday.

That didn't make it any easier to say goodbye to my human life, though.

"Ready, Lolli?" my personal fae guard asked from the kitchen. He was tall, tan, and gorgeous, with dark, wavy hair that was long on the top and short on the sides. Despite his job, he pretty much always wore jogger-style sweatpants and a graphic tee.

He was making eggs and bacon for both of us, even though he'd had to literally pull a pan out of one of my packed boxes to do so.

Cameron Cassette was a pain in my ass. He'd accompanied the bloodwork results that had declared me compatible with fae, and no amount of convincing had gotten him to leave my side. Considering that the Society was paying him to stay, I was stuck with him.

He called me *Lolli*, as in *Lollipop*, because I'd had one in my mouth the first time we met. And it rhymed with my actual name, Molly.

The bastard had invaded my life for four years. He even had his own room in my apartment, which was paid for by the fae Society. I'd tried to argue against that, but they required more security than I could afford.

And no one came out on top in an argument with fae. Some of them had mind magic. The ones who didn't had elemental magic of some kind. Some of them could even shift into dragons and other mystical animals.

"Ready to get away from you," I drawled, adjusting the hem of my oversized sweater. It was the middle of winter and I lived in the mountains, so it was cold and snowy. But honestly, I lived in sweaters even when it was hot, just cranking the AC up during the summer since the bill was on the Society's dime.

My four-sizes-too-big sweater was bright yellow. It had a sarcastic *"good morning, sunshine"* written in scripted letters across the front, with a sun that resembled a skull beneath it. The color wasn't great with my natural blonde hair, but the sweater was my favorite, so I didn't give a damn.

I'd paired it with my comfiest black leggings, and hadn't bothered with makeup. The people in charge of the reality show would cake me in makeup when I got there, whether I liked it or not.

Cam chuckled, but didn't say anything else.

I was sure he was just as ready to escape me. Though we had come to a grudging agreement to be civil, he was the one who spoke for the Society when it came to me.

Which meant he was the one who got to tell me what I was and wasn't allowed to do. And scare away anyone I got too close to.

He hadn't told me much about his life or his past, but he didn't know much of mine either.

At least I was getting away from him.

That reminded me…

I sat up.

"Now that we're going our separate ways, will you tell me what your magic is? You know I'm going into this whole thing blind. No one has given me any details about fae." Everything I knew, I'd learned on the internet. And the internet was about as trustworthy as a compulsive liar who got paid for telling anything but the truth.

"Nope." He didn't so much as consider it.

And he knew what I meant without me elaborating. Every fae did. Their true nature was always hidden from us, because they could all look human.

They didn't look *exactly* human, of course. They were all a little taller than their average human counterparts, coming in around 6'2" or 6'3". And they were unnaturally beautiful, too.

But there were some human guys who fit that profile, so you couldn't assume anything.

I hadn't assumed with Cam. I'd asked.

And he'd told me I'd have to figure it out myself.

I'd tried that, but he refused to tell me if any of my guesses were correct.

I *did* have one clue after all the years I'd been forced to spend with him.

He'd grabbed a hot pan without burning himself once. I didn't know if all fae could do that. If not, he probably had fire magic.

I'd never seen his wings—which all fae had—and if he could shift into an animal form, I'd never seen it.

"Eat up. I don't know when they'll feed you next," he said, setting a plate down on the countertop.

I reluctantly walked over. Though I wasn't hungry, he did have a point. And as much as we weren't friends, I did trust him when it came to having my best interests in mind. He'd never done anything to overstep my boundaries, or to disrespect me, and it had been *years*.

"So are you moving on to guard another compatible mate after this?" I asked him, as I cut into my eggs.

"Something like that." He dished his onto his plate.

"You're being vague again, as usual."

He flashed me a grin. "Am I?"

"Don't put your mind magic anywhere near me," I warned, holding my fork up as if it were a weapon. It wasn't, but he'd play along.

He lifted his hands in surrender. "Wouldn't dream of it."

"Good." I took another bite of my eggs. "You're going to miss me."

"Am I?" The question was repeated.

So was the grin.

I held my fork up in warning again, and he took a large step back. His hands were still raised.

There was a knock at the door, and I sighed.

"Just take the plate with you. I'll handle cleaning this up and making sure your things get to the right place," Cameron said, striding toward the door.

"The right place, meaning, my future mate's house?" I drawled.

I hadn't been told much, but I had been told *that*. No fae in his right mind would move into a small apartment with me.

Except Cam.

But he was the exception. And he was getting paid by the Society to live there, I was sure.

"Yup." He opened the front door and greeted the man on the doorstep. The newcomer was tall, with light brown skin and loose, curly black hair. "Hey, Rhett."

The man grunted in response.

"Good luck, Lollipop," Cam said, stepping back and opening the door wider.

I didn't consider hugging him.

We weren't close like that.

And even if we had been, it was illegal for an unmated fae to touch a compatible human until he was trying to woo her during the game show. I'd never been told why, but it was considered a big deal.

If I'd ever been in real physical danger and he had to touch me in some way to protect me, that would be allowed. Everything else was off limits.

"Thanks. Nice knowing you." I saluted him as I walked out the door, leaving all of my stuff with Cameron. The paperwork I'd received a week earlier made it clear that I wasn't bringing any of my own stuff to the game show.

I followed Rhett down the hall. After we stepped into the elevator, I turned for one last look at the door to my old apartment.

My eyebrows lifted when I saw Cam standing in the doorway, watching me go.

He lifted his hand in a small wave, but the door closed before I could wave back.

"How far is it to the *Bachelorette* mansion?" I asked.

"You're not going to the mansion," Rhett said, his voice gravelly.

My eyebrows shot upward. "What? Where am I going, then?"

"I'm not authorized to say."

My stomach clenched. I grabbed my phone from my pocket and dialed Cameron's number, because I couldn't see any other option.

"Miss me already?"

"Rhett's not taking me to the mansion," I said quickly. "He won't tell me where I'm going. Is this safe? Are you sure he's from the Society?"

"Rhett is like a brother to me. I've known him a lot longer than you've been alive. I trust him. The Society trusts him. Whatever the plans have changed to, he's telling the truth."

I let out a long breath. "You're positive?"

"I wouldn't have let you walk away with him if I wasn't."

As much as I didn't want to, I believed him.

"Alright. Sorry to bother you, I guess."

"You're not a bother."

"Bye." I hung up quickly, biting my lip.

"I'm going to need your phone," Rhett said, as the elevator stopped on the bottom floor.

I started to protest, but the look he leveled at me said it wasn't a request.

So, I handed it over.

He shut it off and tucked it in his pocket before leading me to the armored vehicle I'd expected. That, at least, was normal.

WE DIDN'T DRIVE to the mansion.

We drove to a private airport, instead.

The beauty team I'd been expecting was there.

They'd set up a makeshift studio in a corner of the airport. Rhett gestured me toward the makeup chair before stepping to the side of the room, and a whirlwind began immediately.

Someone started throwing what I thought were highlights in my hair. There was no mirror, but I recognized the bleach and foils from videos I'd seen of people having their hair done.

Someone else did my nails, while another person ran something warm over my face.

Someone forced me to my back and gave me eyelash extensions while someone else washed the bleach from my hair.

Yet another person scrubbed my feet and legs with some kind of exfoliant.

I tried to ask questions whenever I could.

Why weren't we at the mansion, which I knew was only a few hours by car from the city I lived in?

Where was I going?

What was happening?

None of them had a clue. Or if they did, they also weren't *authorized* to tell me.

At least no one brought out any hot wax. Getting a Brazilian in a room full of people would've been nightmare-worthy.

Eventually, all the beauty shit was over, and one of the people led me behind a changing screen. She handed me an olive-green bikini and a pair of ripped cutoff shorts in the same color.

I blinked down at them.

"We're running out of time. Hurry," the woman urged.

"I'm supposed to be going to the *Bachelorette* mansion," I said, my voice uncertain. "I shouldn't need a bikini right now."

"We don't have time for this. If we're not on time, the Society doesn't tip us," the woman said, her voice impatient.

As bad as I felt for that, we were talking about my *life*. My future. I'd just spent two hours getting beautified—I wasn't going to put on a bikini and strut out without at least one answer.

"Tell me why I need to wear this, and I'll put it on," I finally said.

The woman scowled.

I gave her a hard look.

I wasn't budging on that, whatever the consequences were for her. I didn't want her or the rest of the team to lose money, but I needed an answer.

She finally looked around, then took one step closer to me.

Her voice dropped, so I leaned in closer. "You didn't hear this from me, but the Society is starting another game show. Some of the fae aren't interested in *Bachelorette*."

My eyes widened. "And they're starting this with *me*?"

She jerked her head in a nod. "I don't know what it's called or what the premise is. I assume it's another mating thing. All they told us is that you need to be ready for the beach, and we won't be there to fix you up."

"The *beach*?" My voice was tight.

A little frantic.

I hadn't been to a beach since I was ten or eleven. Before the war. Before I lost my parents. Before the fae.

What was I going to do on a beach? And what were we doing that would require being away from humans who could be the beauty crew? The *Bachelorette* girls were always caked in makeup.

Since the fae had already brought back one reality game show revolving around romance, I tried to rake my mind for the names and concepts of others.

But I couldn't come up with one.

And the woman had told me what I needed to know, so I couldn't delay any longer.

I stripped my shoes, favorite sweater, and leggings off and pulled the bikini on. I double-knotted the stupid little string between my tits for security's sake. I didn't have huge boobs, but those suckers weren't small either. And I definitely didn't want the top coming undone.

The strings on both sides of the bottoms got the same treatment. I was still trying to button the tight shorts when the woman tugged me out from behind the screen and dragged my stumbling ass toward a door that led outside.

"I don't have shoes," I protested, giving up on the button and holding the shorts up myself as I struggled to keep up with her.

"You won't need them." She stopped me right beside Rhett, who was waiting in front of a small, private plane. "She's ready," the woman declared.

Ready?

That was definitely not the word I'd use.

"Let go of her *now*." Rhett's voice was calm, but anyone could hear the undercurrent of threat.

"Of course." She dropped my arm, dipped her head in a nod that sort of resembled a bow, then hurried back into the tiny airport.

I hastily fastened the button on my shorts. Not that it helped cover me. My entire damn body was on display. And while I was mostly confident, I did have a few insecurities. Who didn't?

I didn't particularly want any of them blasted on TV, either.

"Can you tell me what's going on now?" I asked Rhett, as he

gestured for me to enter the plane. "Also, can you make sure the stylists get their bonus?"

"They'd get it even if you were late," Rhett rumbled. "The Society doesn't piss humans off when there's another option."

I actually believed him about that. Most humans loved the fae, especially because they got to watch them fall in love with humans on global television.

Which was probably the reason for the game show thing.

Inside the plane, I looked around. It was sleek and modern, not entirely comfortable-looking.

Then again, flying on any normal airline wouldn't have been any more comfortable.

"You didn't answer my first question," I reminded him as I took a seat in a fancy leather chair.

He gestured to my seat belt, and I buckled it.

"I'm not allowed to explain until we're nearly to the island. It's about nine hours away."

Nine hours?

Holy shit.

"Where's the island?" I asked, since that didn't seem to be an illegal topic.

"I don't know." He took his own seat, but didn't buckle up.

I didn't bother telling him to prioritize his safety. He was fae. If the plane started to go down or something, he could just fly off.

"Can I have my phone back?" I asked, hoping I could text Cam just to see if he knew anything about this new game show. As annoying as he was, he was my only actual contact in the fae Society.

"After you're mated."

He handed me the remote to a TV before I had the chance to sigh, so I turned on an action movie to distract myself.

THREE AND A HALF MOVIES LATER, Rhett turned the TV off.

I didn't protest at the sudden interruption.

Finally, he was going to tell me something.

"You're being placed in a new kind of mating game," Rhett said, his gaze on me.

I bit my lip.

Couldn't tell him I'd already learned that.

"It's called *Survival of the Mated*. Many of the rougher, older fae are unwilling to play *Bachelorette*. Or to pursue a woman who is dating another man. Let alone a dozen of them."

I blinked.

Older, rougher fae?

That didn't sound good for me.

"This one is entirely male driven. It's a spin on a game show called *Survivor*, but you aren't truly an active participant in the events. You won't choose your mate until the end, when you select one of the three final contestants."

My eyes widened.

"The men will vote one of your potential mates out on their own every two to three days. You'll have no say in the voting. If you show any particular affinity to one of the guys, he will likely be off the island immediately."

Shit.

Holy shit.

I scrambled mentally to remember the bits and pieces of *Survivor* I'd seen as a kid. I'd watched it with my family, and I could remember the alliances. The scheming. The betrayal.

I wasn't playing Bachelorette... I was playing whatever the hell the opposite of it was.

There would be no developing feelings between me and the guys. No friendship.

Because anyone I showed interest in would get voted off immediately.

I had so little control over who I'd spend my life with, it was horrifying.

"Can't they find someone else to test this out on?" I finally whispered.

"All of the candidates aging out this year were considered, and you were chosen as the best."

"Great." I squeezed my eyes shut.

"It's time to unbuckle and stand up, Molly. We're about to arrive."

"Shouldn't I stay buckled before the plane lands?" I asked.

"Not this time." He unbuckled the belt, and I stood reluctantly. "Close your eyes and hold your arms out."

I did as commanded.

A heavy bag was set on my shoulders, and I stumbled a little.

"Now, brace yourself," he said.

My forehead creased with my frown, and my eyes opened.

Before I could ask why, he grabbed the back of the bag he'd buckled me into, opened the plane's door, and tossed me through it.

MOLLY

I SCREAMED until my throat was raw.

A parachute deployed itself after a few seconds of free-falling, but I couldn't stop screaming.

Heights—I didn't like heights.

Not even a little.

My third-story apartment had been too high for me. I left the curtains closed 99% of the time.

Skydiving?

And without warning?

It was hell.

When my feet finally hit the sand, my legs were so shaky that my knees buckled and I crashed to the ground. It was soft and white, but I didn't notice the color or feel of it against my spread palms.

My chest was rising and falling too rapidly, my panic so thick I could smell and taste it.

I heard someone land beside me, but couldn't look over.

"You're fine, Molly," Rhett said beside me.

I wanted to tell him to go to hell.

Or claw his eyes out with my fingernails.

But I couldn't manage to get myself off the sand.

"The other men will be arriving soon. You'll want to compose yourself. The cameras are rolling, and there's only so much they can cut out in editing."

"Shut. Up." I barely managed to grit the words out.

He did as I commanded, though.

I gave myself three seconds to stay where I was before I finally let out a slow, long breath and lifted myself to my knees.

My abdomen was so tight it hurt.

I let myself take three more breaths before I stood.

My legs shook.

There was sand plastered to basically all of my exposed skin. The unexposed skin, too.

But I managed to stand. The backpack on my shoulders was insanely heavy, though, making it hard to stay steady.

"There are three buckles on the front," Rhett said. When I glanced over at him, I found him shirtless, with a pair of massive, wings spread behind his back. They looked like they were made of glass, and were entirely clear. He was a few inches taller, too. And thick horns protruded from his scalp.

My hands shook as I undid them. "You're a real bastard. Who *throws* someone out of a plane?"

I stumbled forward when the weight crashed down behind me, finally leaving me free. He grabbed my upper arm to catch me before I could fall again. "Just following Society instructions."

"You and the Society can both kiss my ass."

"We'll leave that for your mate."

If I hadn't already been sweating, my face would've flushed.

My mate, who I wasn't *really* going to get to choose. Every other compatible human had free will when it came to their game show. They could choose any of the supernatural men.

But me?

I'd get three options.

The three who either outsmarted or outplayed the rest in some way.

In all likelihood, the three I liked the *least*.

"This is bullshit," I said, brushing sand off my boobs, tiny bikini, and shorts, but barely making a dent.

Damn, I hated sand.

It was going to be a long month.

I really hoped there was some kind of a shelter built. Or at least some wood for the guys to build something with. The last thing I wanted to do was spend my nights on the sand.

Actually, the last thing I wanted to do was spend my nights snuggled between gigantic fae guys in a tiny shelter, on the sand.

Sure, they'd be attractive, but snuggling would give them ideas.

Maybe sand wasn't *that* bad.

Another small plane made its way toward us, the sound getting louder as it approached.

"I could refuse to mate with any of these guys," I said. "If the Society wants to play hardball by throwing me out of a plane and into a whole new game, I can just decide not to play."

Rhett snorted.

It was the first sign of emotion I'd seen from him.

"You're about to be secluded on an island with a dozen horny, lonely, *dying* fae males. Any of them could overpower you with little more than the blink of an eye. I've been assigned to protect you while you're here, but if you don't do your job, I'm under no obligation to do mine."

My chest tightened. "You'd let me die?"

He laughed.

Loudly.

"No one coming here would ever let that happen. We need you. If I don't protect you, you'll end up at the center of a physical battle. The winner will claim you, permanently. And I can promise you won't like him."

I didn't need his promise.

I was pretty damn confident of *that* myself.

Which meant I either had to play along, or accept a hellish mate bond that would literally last forever as it made both me and the other guy immortal.

Sand was actually starting to look nice.

"I want Cameron back," I said flatly.

"He's done guarding."

Before I could ask what he meant, the plane flew over us.

My heartbeat picked up as I saw the first guy jump out.

He wasn't in his human form.

His gorgeous, feathery-white wings were spread out behind him, his dark skin on display thanks to his bare chest. His head sported a pair of thick horns.

The second man followed.

His wings were gossamer, resembling glass like Rhett's, but with a mixture of colors in them unlike my new guard's.

The third came after him, then the fourth, and so on, until there were twelve men flying toward us and the plane was leaving.

"I'd like to quit now," I whispered to Rhett.

"So would I."

I started to flash him a glare, but the first man landed before I got the chance.

My head whipped back to that direction.

Toward the ocean.

Way too close to me.

I wanted to take a few steps back, but Rhett's hand was still on my arm. As if he thought I might try to run away.

Yeah, right.

There was nowhere to go.

And even if there was, I had no doubt the dozen winged fae would catch me quickly. I wasn't fast.

The rest of the guys landed one after another.

They were all in their fae forms, a few inches taller than their usual human forms. All of them had horns, though there was a variety of horn and wing shapes.

Hopefully *that* was what Rhett meant when he said horny, because I wasn't interested in sleeping with half a dozen different guys like some of the *Bachelorette* chicks did. I wasn't even sure I wanted to sleep with *one*.

I'd had sex twice before the world nearly ended, and it really hadn't impressed me. My vibrator worked better than any man I'd ever met.

"Line up," Rhett said.

His voice wasn't raised, but the men followed the command anyway. The woman's guard was always sort of the host in *Bachelorette*, so it seemed safe to assume he was taking that role in *Survival of the Mated*.

The men stepped into place, forming a line. All of them were bare chested, which seemed required with the wings spread out behind them.

In *Bachelorette*, they stayed in their human forms.

Just the sight of them with their massive sizes, wings, and horns was enough to make me fight a shiver.

I didn't let myself look too closely at the line of them. Whoever I paid attention to seemed likely to become an immediate target, so I'd avoid looking at anyone until I figured out a plan.

"Welcome to Survival of the Mated," Rhett said. "You all know the rules. No killing. No using magic on the female without her permission. And no starting a bond with her. Beginning a mate bond before winning is a death sentence."

I bit the inside of my cheek.

That hadn't been mentioned before.

How would a person even start a mate bond? I had an impressively small amount of information, considering my situation.

"Now, meet the female you're competing for." Rhett gestured to me. "She'll introduce herself."

I blinked.

On *Bachelorette*, there was no introduction. There were just... dates.

But I wasn't on *Bachelorette*.

And I needed to figure out a way to get my head in the game. Whatever the game was.

Which meant an introduction.

So I let out a quick breath and forced myself to act like I wasn't absolutely terrified. The more casual I could act and the more human I could seem, the more I hoped they would realize that I wasn't just a prize to be won as part of their new game show.

"I'm Molly Maye," I said. "I'm twenty-four. I have an accounting degree. It's boring, but stable. Unlike this." I gestured to myself, the guys, and the island. "I worked full-time before I was dragged here. I like to eat desserts. Don't like to exercise. Also, I don't like sand."

One or two of the guys chuckled.

The sound was kind of familiar, but I figured that was just my nerves making me imagine things.

"The guys will introduce themselves after the game begins," Rhett said. "The first challenge starts now. There are a dozen survival packs hidden in the jungle. Each of you can only retrieve one. The last one back loses the chance to vote the first man off the island tomorrow night. The one who finds the pack with the weapons in it spends an hour on a boat with Molly as soon as it ends."

A moment of tense silence passed.

"Any questions?" Rhett asked.

It seemed pretty simple.

The guys had to find survival packs. The slowest one lost their vote. The one who found the right bag won a reward.

Me being the reward was shitty, but expected.

"Go," he said, and hell broke loose.

Sand sprayed in the air as wings flapped and fae took off. I closed my eyes against the barrage, but was too slow. They were already stinging, and gritty.

When I opened them again, I could hear yelling in the distance. A few guys were flying in the air above the jungle.

One man was still walking there. His body position was casual, and there was something about his figure that I kind of recognized.

The golden wings on his back and horns on his head made me feel stupid for feeling that, though. Obviously, I didn't recognize any of the fae.

"How long is this going to take?" I asked Rhett.

There were no chairs to sit on.

I spotted a camera drone flying off to my left, recording both of us, and resisted the urge to flip the Society off through it.

They probably wouldn't see it if I did.

And all it could do was piss them off, which seemed pointless.

The camera drones were made with some kind of techy camouflaging that made them difficult to spot, but I'd read a few articles about how to find them.

"Depends how bloody it gets," Rhett said.

I grimaced. "How bad do you think it'll get?"

"Very."

"Care to elaborate?"

"Seems pretty simple. The man who spends the first hour with you will have a big advantage."

"He'll also be a target, won't he?"

"It's likely. But at the same time, they're all going to be doing everything they can to win you over. Even if they make it to the end, they can't win without you choosing them over the others. A reward with you will be the most neutral way to get to know you."

"Lovely."

"Yep." Rhett stared out at the trees.

I did too.

I THOUGHT we'd have to wait a while, but it was less than five minutes later that the first man emerged. He was flying, with tan wings spread behind him as he soared toward us.

"Who's that?" I whispered to Rhett.

"I'm not allowed to give you information or opinions."

I sighed. "You're useless to me."

"Want me to hand you over to them?"

I scowled at him, but he continued staring out at the trees.

The man was basically a sarcastic brick wall.

Tan-winged guy landed. He had bronze skin, a gleaming white smile, and the smallest horns on any of the men I'd seen. Up close, his wings almost looked... furry?

Odd.

Another guy emerged from the trees behind him, but the first was already offering me his hand, like he wanted a handshake.

Despite my discomfort, I shook his hand.

His grip was too firm, but I managed not to wince.

"Nice to meet you, Molly. I'm Kaden. I also hate sand."

"It sucks," I agreed, not sure what else to say.

Another man approached.

He shot Kaden a narrow-eyed look before looking at me. His hair was white, his skin was pale, his wings were gossamer, and his eyes were multicolored in a way that made me feel like he was staring into my soul.

"Hello, Molly Maye," he said. "I am Oren."

"Hi." Something about him made me uncomfortable, but I wasn't about to say that aloud. Seemed like a sure-fire way to get him to the end.

Two more guys joined the group.

They were polite, but I forgot their names as quickly as they said them. Neither of them creeped me out, at least.

Kaden was chatting to me about his house—a huge beach house, which was truly ironic considering how he'd intro-duced himself—when I heard one of the other guys call out,

"Did you survive the dogpile, Cam?"

My body stiffened.

It couldn't be *my* Cam.

...Could it?

He chuckled.

The sound was so familiar, it sent goosebumps down my arms.

"Didn't bother going near it," he said.

I spun around, cutting Kaden off entirely.

My brown eyes collided with a pair of familiar greens. It was Cameron, but... different.

Fae.

Really fae.

His horns were massive, his thick, golden wings spread out behind him. All he had on was a pair of basketball shorts instead of his usual joggers. His lack of a shirt revealed a few tattoos on his chest and shoulder that I'd never seen before.

"Cameron?"

I wasn't sure whether to be stunned or angry. Either way, it caught me off guard.

"Hey, Lolli." He flashed me a grin.

It was easier-going than the last one I'd gotten.

Lazier.

The words and tone settled my uncertainty.

I was stunned, but I was *furious*.

"What the hell are you doing here?" I demanded. "Did you know you were coming before I left?"

"I did." He gave me a playful grimace. "Sorry."

My anger rose.

Three more guys joined us, and though they were bleeding, I barely noticed them. Definitely didn't greet them.

"You stood there and made me breakfast, knowing you were joining me on the island this afternoon?"

"Technically, it was yesterday."

"I'm confused," one of the guys behind me said.

"You and me both," I snapped.

"I was assigned to guard Lolli for the past few years," Cameron explained. "Got the letter last week that I was chosen for the game. Didn't realize we weren't doing the *Bachelorette* thing until then, either."

"But you *did* realize and decide not to tell me," I shot back.

"Did I?"

"Oh, fuck off, Cam."

Thankfully, some big, burly bastard came swooping into the group with a loud "Whoop!" before anymore arguing went down.

"I've got the weapons!" he declared, wearing a massive grin as he strode through the crowd toward me. There was blood on his hands and splattered over his knuckles and chest. He was tan and blond, with big, black scaly wings spread out behind him. His hair was shaved completely on the sides but long on top, and I had a feeling it was usually styled perfectly.

I took two steps sideways in hopes of avoiding him.

The man had at least an inch on all the other guys, except maybe Rhett. He could absolutely squash me.

My movement was useless, because the guy just took two gigantic steps up to my side and grabbed my hand, lifting it in the air. The blood on his fists made my fingers slick.

I cringed and tried to lean away.

He just grinned wider.

"You're mine for the next hour, Dolly," he declared.

I flashed Rhett a desperate look.

The one he gave me back said the guy wasn't hurting me in any way, so I was on my own.

"It's Molly, Asshole," one of the other guys grumbled.

I tried like hell to free my hand from Asshole's grasp while he dragged me to the little speedboat Rhett had pointed out to us.

Rhett shifted into his wings and horns, the gorgeous, glassy appendages out behind him as he followed us overhead.

three

MOLLY

ASSHOLE COULDN'T STOP TALKING about himself.

I swear, he was trying to sell himself to me like one of those obnoxious salesmen who doesn't listen to what the customer wants or needs.

Oh, and his name was actually Kyle.

Though he *did* seem like an asshole, so the shoe fit.

While he talked and I pretended to be listening to the details about his life, my mind kept returning to the real problem:

Cameron Cassette.

I'd thought I could trust him.

Learning otherwise hurt.

It really fucking hurt.

And even more than that, it made me wonder what the point was. If I couldn't trust a fae I'd spent four years literally living with, could I ever learn to trust the one I ended up mated to?

They just wanted their immortality. They didn't care about us little humans.

Eventually, the boat returned to the beach, and we climbed out. Asshole offered his hand to help me stay balanced. I couldn't think of a good enough reason to turn him down, so I accepted.

The rest of the men had already started working on—you guessed it—the shelter I'd been wondering about. A quick glance told me there was no wood, nails, or anything else to help build it.

So, we were using bamboo and woven leaves and vines.

It was going to be *great*.

None of the men had put shirts on, but it was insanely hot, so that didn't surprise me. It wasn't like anyone had extra clothes anyway.

I was so sticky with sweat that getting all the sand off my skin had become a pipe dream.

I went through the pitiful pile of survival supplies we'd been given. There was a shit-ton of sunblock, a few cans of food, and a small bag of rice, which was good. But everything else?

Junk.

Literally.

We had four boxes of ice cream. The guys had eaten what they could salvage of those while I was on the crappiest date of my life. Whatever hadn't been eaten was not only melted, but hot, thanks to the island's temperature.

On top of the ice cream, there was candy.

Boxes and bags of melted, gooey gummy candy.

In most situations, I could easily eat as much candy as your average four-year-old on Halloween. My supply of lollipops had taken up almost an entire box when I was packing. But on a deserted island, when it was just melted goo?

I'd pass.

The guys I hadn't met yet tried to casually take turns coming up to me. They introduced themselves and asked how I was doing, stuff like that. It was kind of awkward, but I could tell they were trying to be nice and friendly.

One of the last few to come up to me was one of the ones who'd introduced himself to me earlier. I still couldn't remember his name. He had pale skin and blond hair, and didn't look kind.

He reintroduced himself as Julian as he sat down beside me and started weaving palm fronds with me. It was monotonous, but something to keep my mind somewhat distracted from the heat and exactly where I was.

"What happened between you and Cameron?" the guy asked me. I tried not to stare at his glass-like wings too much. There were swirls of color in them that kept drawing my attention.

"I'm sure you got the gist of it earlier."

"That's the full story?"

"We've been at odds ever since he showed up with my blood results and announced he was my guard," I said. "Not telling me about this was just the icing on the cake."

"Has he ever mentioned wanting you?"

I flashed him a dark look. "Of course not. We don't get along."

He dipped his head. "It's just strange."

"What do you mean?"

"Cameron is friends with everyone. He's one of the few old unmated fae who doesn't hold grudges or hate anyone."

"He's old?"

"Yeah. Won't live much longer without taking a mate."

My throat constricted slightly. "Why didn't he go on *Bachelorette*, then?"

Julian shrugged. "Probably the possessiveness, but I never asked."

The possessive bit didn't make sense, so it went in one ear and out the next.

But I had never asked him either.

Maybe I should.

I'd assumed he was young and had plenty of time. I didn't know how long fae lived without taking mates to ensure the immortality thing, but had assumed they'd physically look aged as they approached the end of their lives.

Guess I'd assumed wrong.

"Well he's obviously not winning this game," I said.

Julian chuckled and didn't say anything else.

It was kind of nice that he didn't try to sell himself to me or convince me how great he was. Made it seem more like he wanted to see if he was interested in me before pushing.

Or maybe he just realized that me choosing between the last three contestants wasn't much of a choice, and thought he'd have the upper hand if he let me breathe when the other guys didn't.

Everyone probably had an ulterior motive.

But that thought made me wonder if Cameron did. Because Cam? The guy had to be thinking *something*. He wasn't a moron.

And if he wasn't interested in winning the contest or just seeing what happened to me, he wouldn't be on the island. Period.

But what did that mean for me?

I had no idea.

. . .

MY BODY and stomach both ached fiercely by the time the sun finally set. The temperature dropped when it did.

Exhaustion had set in hours earlier, but our shelter was made of bamboo, and looked the opposite of comfortable. So, even when the guys told me to rest, I kept weaving palm fronds.

Someone cooked all the rice and most of the vegetables while I was making a visit to the place we'd designated as the bathroom (no, it did not smell grand), so that was shitty.

Everyone only got a few bites of food.

A few of the guys offered me their portion, Cam not included, but I politely turned them down.

The last thing I wanted was to owe a debt to someone on that island.

I tried not to, but couldn't stop myself from noticing when Cameron slipped away after dinner. Some of the fae guys were barraging me with questions about my life, and didn't want to take no for an answer.

Though I played along for a while, my frustration grew when they refused to leave me alone, and I finally made a show of saying that I needed to use the bathroom for a few minutes. Alone.

I must've sounded almost as annoyed as I felt, because the men let me go.

Rhett would follow me at a distance to keep me safe, so it wasn't like it was dangerous for me to abandon the group and the campfire.

As soon as I was out of the group's view, I headed in another direction, toward a part of the beach I hadn't seen anyone explore yet. Most people had been sticking close to each other all day—and close to me too.

When I stepped through the trees and onto the stretch of beach, I stopped.

It wasn't as empty as I'd thought.

Cameron was sitting on his ass, sprawled out on the sand and staring at the ocean.

Part of me wanted to turn around and walk back to the fire. The angry part.

The frustrated part of me wanted to find my own beach to sit down quietly on.

But the confused, hurt parts of me?

They propelled me across the sand.

My footsteps were quiet, and Rhett remained in the trees when I made my way to Cameron's side.

"Hey, Loll." His voice was quiet, but upbeat as I sat down next to him.

I didn't reply to that.

I didn't know what to say.

A minute of tense silence went by before I finally spoke. "Why didn't you tell me?"

"It was against the rules. The Society was very clear that if I told you anything about the new game or my presence here, I wouldn't be coming. Considering they can read minds, they would know if I broke that rule."

"Why did you even want to come?" My voice rose slightly.

He chuckled. "The same reason the rest of these bastards are here."

"You want a mate."

"Do I?"

"Stop. I'm not dealing with your avoidance anymore. Answer my questions honestly, or walk away."

He let out a long breath. "Habit. Sorry."

I shook my head. "Julian told me you're dying."

"Of course he did."

"Why didn't you go on *Bachelorette*? We both know you could talk just about any of those women into mating with you. You're charming when you want to be."

He chuckled. "If I gave a damn about any of those women, maybe I would've."

"What does that mean?" I frowned.

"I've lived a long time. Even without mating, fae don't have short lives. I'd rather die with my freedom than tie myself permanently to a woman I didn't want."

My forehead creased further. "If you want to say something, just say it."

"I have connections. More than any of the other guys here. I knew I'd be fighting for you before we ever met, Lolli. And I was always going to play to win. Guarding was just a way to get to know you first."

Holy shit.

Holy *shit*.

What was I supposed to do with that information?

"I can admit the island caught me off guard. No one told me we'd be starting a new game show until I got the invitation letter last week," he added. "But when I did, I put together a plan."

"Care to enlighten me?"

He flashed me a grin. In the moonlight, his green eyes were brighter than usual, and his teeth glinted white. His hair was a mess, and his gigantic horns were definitely eye-catching, but it was the golden wings that really made me stare. "What'll you give me if I do?"

I scoffed. "Less hatred?"

"You don't hate me." His voice was amused. "I'm the only man on this island you trust."

"How could I possibly trust you? You lied to me. And apparently, you've been planning to marry me since the first moment we met." I tossed a hand toward the ocean. "For all I know, you've been altering my mind to make me like you since then. Doesn't exactly scream *trustworthy*."

"I don't have that kind of magic, Lolli. The fae with the delicate-looking wings are the ones with mental power. The rest of us are elemental. All our power is physical."

"What's your element, then?"

"Fire." One of his wings stretched out behind me, and soft flames licked up the golden feathers. I couldn't help but stare.

The warmth felt so good that I found myself leaning closer to him.

"Damn," I said. "How do I know the mental magic thing is true?"

"Ask any of the other guys. They have no reason to lie about it."

"I've seen you talking to them, though. They like you."

"Like I said, I have a plan."

"One that involves lying to me?"

He chuckled. "No. I'll never have to do that again."

They shouldn't have, but the words eased my worry a bit. "I should probably go. Someone will come looking for me soon."

"You've got a little more time. You were getting irritated long before I left. Even the stupidest of them would've picked up on it by the time you walked away. None of them want to be on your bad side, so they'll give you space until they have a reason to be suspicious."

"And me being alone with you isn't a reason?"

He grinned at me again. "They don't know we're together. And I'm not on anyone's radar as a threat."

He was probably right.

Everyone thought I hated him. And I kind of did.

But I also still kind of trusted him. Which was obviously a problem.

Wasn't it?

"What do you want in exchange for telling me your plan?" I asked, staring out at the ocean so I wouldn't have to meet his gaze again.

He considered it for a moment before answering.

"A hug."

"A hug?" I lifted an eyebrow in his direction.

"Yup. You've never hugged me, because of the rules. I want to experience it."

I snorted. "I'm sure you've hugged a woman before. It won't be any different than that."

"Compatible mates smell different." He lifted a shoulder. "Take it or leave it."

I looked back at the water. "How long does the hug have to be?"

"I don't know. Not short. Not endless either, for obvious reasons."

Obvious reasons being that we were on a deserted island with eleven other guys who wanted to make me their mate.

"You'll have to let me burn my scent off you afterward, too," he added. "If you smell like me, they'll realize we were together."

I considered it.

A hug for a confession.

It did sound reasonable. Reasonable for me, at least. He didn't really have anything to gain from telling me his plan. If I didn't like it, I could probably do something to hurt it.

And a hug wasn't exactly a huge ask.

"Alright," I agreed. "A hug for a plan."

"I'll tell you after you pay up."

I agreed, stood up, and brushed sand off my ass. Though I expected him to stand too, he remained where he was.

When I frowned, he beckoned me toward him.

I rolled my eyes, but sat down on his lap. I didn't consider that I'd be straddling him until my legs were on either side of his hips, and I was looking him square in the eyes.

His body was warm.

I wanted to lean in closer, and we *had* made a deal.

So, I wrapped my arms around his neck and pressed my chest against his.

He took in a long, deep breath as I pressed my body closer, hugging him. His arms went around my back, and his warmth seeped into my bare skin.

He felt good.

Really, really good.

I felt him harden beneath me, but didn't comment on it. I was getting a little turned on by the contact, and didn't want him mentioning *that*.

"I'm sorry they threw you out of a plane," he murmured. "If I'd known that was coming, I would've made sure it didn't happen."

My eyes stung. "Yeah, that was terrifying."

"I know." His hand moved over my back, the touch slow but calming somehow.

I didn't want to let go of him. Didn't want the hug to end.

"Tell me your plan before I regret sitting on you," I mumbled.

He chuckled, his body rumbling against mine.

That felt nice.

"The Society refused to let me tell you anything, so I knew you'd be pissed when you saw me, and used it to my advantage. Most of the guys think you hate me now. A few of them are smart enough to realize I might be playing into that on purpose, but I'll ally with the stupid ones to make sure the suspicious are gone first. By the time they realize what I've done, I'll already have won the game."

"Assuming I pick you in the end."

"You know you'll survive living with me. Can you say the same about anyone else?" he countered.

I couldn't.

"Better the devil you know than the one you don't?" I asked. "Seems like a risky thing to make a bet on."

"Lolli," he said, humor in his voice. "I'm making a bet on *you*. And you can be damn sure it's not one I'm going to lose."

As much as I was uncertain, I *did* believe him.

I just didn't know how to feel about it.

"And what if I tell someone else about your plan?" I finally asked.

"You could," he agreed. "But you have no guarantee they'll be any better than me. All of the bastards on this island are old, and mean. If I thought any of them could treat you better than I can, I'd let them have you. But they don't know you like I do—and they don't have your best interests in mind like me."

"I want to believe you," I said, fully aware of the fact that my body was still pressed against his.

And that my bikini bottoms were getting slightly wet over the certainty in his voice as he talked about treating me well.

If I'd had any reason to think he'd be a doting mate, maybe I would've kissed him too. But I didn't know him well enough for that.

I did know that he would protect me, though.

And I told myself that was why I wasn't pulling away.

"You'll get there." He dragged his hand over my lower back, and my hips arched just a little. "If you do decide to work with me, you can make the plan even better."

"How would I do that?"

"Be vocal about disliking me, but not too vocal. Spend extra time with the guys who may be on to me, to make them bigger targets."

"Who are the first targets, then?" I asked.

"Julian and Kaden."

Julian was the smart, blond one I'd spoken to while weaving the fronds. He had mental magic, if Cam was telling the truth.

Kaden was the one with the furry wings who'd been back first during the challenge. Which meant his magic was elemental.

"They'd be the first to realize what you're planning?"

"Yes. Julian is smart. He knows I wouldn't be here unless I was planning on winning. Might not realize the extent of my plan, but he realizes something's up. We need to get him off the island first."

I bit my lip. "He was asking me questions about us earlier."

Cameron nodded, his head moving lightly against mine. "I assumed he would. You need to keep up the façade of being pissed at me."

"I *am* still pissed at you."

He chuckled. "Keep telling yourself that." He brushed a few strands of hair from my eyes. "I wanted to hold you like this every night in our apartment."

My face flushed. "You did not."

"I did. You don't have to believe me; I'll prove it to you."

"Sure you will."

"I will."

A thought occurred to me. "What if someone reads our minds and realizes the plan?"

"Mental magic is prohibited here, but Julian and Ev are the only telepaths. I can't see either of them risking their position to try to figure out my plan or read your mind. Ev will be high on the priority list to remove because of his magic, just in case. Julian will be gone before he can do any damage."

It was my turn to nod. "How physical should I be when I'm trying to make it seem like I'm into them?"

His arms tightened around me, just slightly. If I hadn't been so aware of his body, I probably wouldn't have noticed it. "Not physical at all. Just spend extra time with them."

"That might work in the beginning, but I can't imagine it will in the long run," I countered. "And the shelter is tiny. Plus, we don't have any blankets. I'm going to have to sleep next to someone."

"You sleep next to me." His voice was edged with something I hadn't heard before.

Something *gravelly*.

I had no idea what the sound was, or what to do about it. It wasn't like I spent much time in close proximity to men. Definitely not enough to tell what he was thinking.

"Sleeping next to you would ruin your whole plan, Cam. I'm supposed to hate you."

His grip tightened, but he didn't disagree.

"I'll sleep next to Julian tonight, since he's your first target," I said. "It's freezing outside, so I'll have to snuggle up with *someone*. I can go with Rhett if you'd rather, but—"

"I don't want you snuggled up with *anyone*." His words came out a definite, clear growl.

It made me shiver a little. I wasn't sure whether that was from nerves or because the sound was kind of sexy.

"It's not avoidable."

His head snapped to the side. "Someone's coming."

I landed on my ass a heartbeat later, and hot flames licked my skin for a moment. The touch was so light, it didn't burn me, though it did warm me.

"I'll have to sleep in the forest," he said, his voice low as he stood up and tucked his hands in his pockets. "I'd lose my fucking mind watching you cuddle up with any of these bastards."

"You'll have to figure it out," I warned.

"Come on, Lollipop," Cam protested, raising his voice. The sudden change in his mood and tone were enough to tell me he was putting on a show for whoever was coming. "Give me a chance to explain."

"I don't want to hear a word from you," I shot back. "I came out here for a few minutes of privacy. Just leave me alone, Asshole."

He winked at me, lifting his hands up by his head as if in surrender. "Alright, alright. I'm walking away."

"Finally."

He strode off the beach in the other direction.

I huffed like I was angry and turned back toward the ocean,

remaining where I was for a few more minutes. My mind replayed my conversation and hug with Cameron.

I wasn't sure what to think or how to feel about all of it. Honestly, I was shocked that he was even interested in mating with me. I really hadn't thought he liked me.

When I started shivering a couple minutes later, I decided it was time to head back to the shelter for some awkward snuggling.

MOLLY

CAM DIDN'T MAKE a reappearance that night.

Not when I whisper-asked Julian if I could sleep next to him to stay warm.

Not when Kyle, the obnoxious dragon asshole from earlier claimed my other side and scooted too close to me.

Not when I eventually managed to fall asleep despite the discomfort of being pressed against bare-chested strangers. They'd put their wings away, but still.

Cam didn't even show up again in the morning when I slipped out of bed while the rest of the guys were still sleeping.

Though I wanted to track him down or go back to our part of the beach, I just sat down next to the fire for warmth. The fae guys had definitely kept me from shivering, but that didn't ease the physical and mental discomfort of spending the night in the arms of men I didn't know or want.

As I sat there, my mind went back to the night before.

To the way I'd sat on Cameron's lap.

The way he hugged me.

His plan to win the game.

I bit my lip.

Could he really do it? He seemed to think he could, even if I didn't help him. And I'd seen the way the other guys talked to him. All of them liked him.

If anyone was creating alliances in the game, they'd want to work with him. I'd made him into everyone's first choice when I yelled at him the day before. He was the one man on the island that no one thought was a threat to win the game.

No one except Julian.

And whoever else was at the top of Cam's hit list.

But did that mean I wanted to help him?

I thought back to the way I'd felt in his arms the night before.

Warm.

Safe.

It was much better than the discomfort I'd had when pinned between Kyle and Julian.

Which made the choice pretty simple.

I was going with Cam's plan.

That didn't mean I had to mate with him. Working with him could mean having some sway over who left and who stayed, which could be to my advantage.

Maybe there was a guy I'd like more than Cameron. I could use the situation to make it work with him, instead.

The more I thought about it, the more upbeat I felt.

I wasn't as helpless as I'd thought.

I DIDN'T GET much solitude by the fire before a guy came up and sat down beside me. He was one of the quieter ones, and his name was Reid. His wings looked delicate, which meant he was one of the fae with mental magic.

Assuming Cam had told me the truth about that.

He didn't speak up when he took a seat, so I didn't either. He looked almost as tired as I did.

"Can I ask you something?" I murmured to him, after a few minutes of comfortable silence.

"Sure." Reid's words were as quiet as mine. Maybe quieter.

"Why do all of you have different wings?" I gestured toward the shelter and all the guys sleeping there. The majority of them had gone back to their human forms the evening before, so there weren't a lot of wings on display for once.

I wanted him to confirm what Cam had said, but I hadn't wanted to come right out and ask.

"The appearance of our wings is determined by the type of our magic," he said. "Mental fae have translucent wings like mine. Elemental fae have opaque, and the different styles correspond to their elements."

So Cam had told me the truth.

"What about the horns?"

"They grow in like hair. All of us have them in our fae forms, and they don't signify anything."

Another guy joined us by the fire.

He sat uncomfortably close to me, so I was pretty sure it was Kyle even before I looked over.

Yep.

Kyle.

"What are we talking about?" His voice was bleary, but loud enough that he'd probably woken up everyone who was still sleeping.

"Magic," Reid said, still talking quietly.

"You didn't tell her about the shifting, did you?" Kyle asked, loud once again.

The other guy sighed.

The sigh was answer enough.

He hadn't wanted me to know about the shifting, whatever that meant.

So, I obviously needed to know what it was.

Two more guys sat down beside us. One was Oren, who still gave me the creeps. The other was Chris, with the white feathery wings.

"What shifting?" I asked.

"We shift between human and fae forms," Kyle said quickly.

That was true, but he was clearly trying to conceal the full truth from me.

I glared at him and scooted multiple inches away. "Don't bullshit me."

Chris chuckled. "Elemental fae have three forms. Human, fae, and beast."

"Beast?" My voice rose slightly.

I'd seen videos of dragons and a few other kinds of magical creatures, so I'd figured that was coming.

But still, it was a big deal.

"We can shift into animals," he agreed. "Air fae become griffins. Water become dragons. Earth become perytons. Fire become phoenixes."

I couldn't remember what a griffin was, exactly. And I didn't think I'd ever heard of a peryton before.

"It takes a shit-ton of energy," Kyle interrupted. "We rarely shift into beast form. Usually wrecks us for a few days afterward."

His green scaly wings told me he must've been a water fae, which was a dragon.

Cameron had to be a phoenix, but I'd never seen him *wrecked* before. Did that mean he hadn't shifted into his beast form since he started guarding me? I'd have to ask.

"Does it take a lot of energy to shift between human and fae?" I wondered.

"Nah. Just a little," Kyle said.

"We need to find something to eat," Julian said, as he joined us by the fire. Three more were behind him. Cam followed them in, like he hadn't been sleeping away from everyone. "We're out of food, unless we count the melted gummy candy."

"The water fae need to go fishing," Kaden, the guy with furry wings, announced.

Kyle scoffed at him. "I'm not wasting my energy like that."

A few heads turned toward the only other guy on the island with scaly wings.

"Come on, Jim," one of the guys said.

Jim looked at me. "What do I get in exchange?"

My irritation rose.

Kyle scooted closer to me.

"Back off," I snapped at him.

He blinked.

I stood.

Though I was frustrated, I wasn't so frustrated that I couldn't put Cam's plan into action a little further.

I strode to Julian's side and folded my arms. Though I didn't touch him in any way, the statement seemed pretty clear. I didn't trust Kyle, but I did trust Julian.

Or at least, I wanted everyone to think I did.

I said, "I'm not giving anyone anything for keeping all of us alive. You bastards knew what you were signing up for when you joined this show. I didn't. I'm not considering anyone who doesn't contribute as a potential mate."

A moment of silence passed.

"I'm going," Jim finally grumbled.

"I'll go too. I should be able to help a little," Chris said.

"Fine," Kyle grunted.

The other guy with golden wings stepped up to Cam's side and whispered, "Want to bet we could bring home twice as much fish as them?"

Cameron grinned at him, and the two of them headed off after the other guys without so much as a glance in my direction.

It was hard to believe that was the same guy whose lap I'd sat on the night before.

And I had to try not to think about *that*, because it gave me feelings I didn't know what to do with.

I went back to weaving palm fronds while everyone else refocused on the shelter, firewood, and such.

The morning passed slowly.

We had fish for lunch. It wasn't enjoyable, and we were all still hungry when the poor creatures had been reduced to bones.

But it was better than nothing.

The rest of the day was filled with small talk, and me sticking with Julian whenever possible.

I ate next to him.

I went looking for firewood with him.

I walked to the water well with him.

And the way everyone had their eyes narrowed at him by the end of the day told me that Cameron's plan was working exactly the way he wanted it to.

JULIAN and I were at the back of the group when it came time to walk to the voting portion of the island. "You're sticking to me on purpose," he said, studying me as we followed the others.

"I trust you more than I trust them," I lied.

"You have no reason to."

"You just seem trustworthy." I wrapped my arms around my middle, itching for a sweatshirt or something. I was so tired of wearing my stupidly small bikini and shorts. It was way too much skin on display for all the shirtless dudes around me. And too much skin that would come in contact with theirs when bedtime came around again.

The only person I hadn't minded with was Cameron.

But I wasn't letting myself think about that.

"If that was true, you wouldn't be so evident about it. You know you're making me a target," Julian said.

I feigned surprise and took a line from Cam's book, answering with a question. "Am I?"

We reached the voting area before he could ask me anything else.

I remembered intricate sets designed for the original *Survivor* show, but the fae Society hadn't bothered with that. They just set up a bunch of logs in a circle, and put a stack of papers and markers next to the fire in the center.

Everyone took a seat.

There was no talking or last-minute drama.

Rhett passed out papers and markers to everyone but me. They all wrote a name down, then passed their votes in.

He showed the votes one by one.

Julian

Julian

Kyle

Julian

Julian

Julian

Julian

Julian

Julian

Julian

Julian

There were twelve men, but one guy had lost his vote in the first challenge, so only eleven votes.

Julian dipped his head toward me before strolling away in the direction opposite the one we'd arrived in.

His voice entered my mind for a moment, and I sucked in a sharp breath at the sudden intrusion.

"Well-played, Molly. Good luck."

Everyone's eyes were on me when I refocused on where I was, and realized I was still seated while they were all standing.

"Thought I saw a spider," I said weakly.

Kyle reached for my arm, about to pull me up, but I was on my feet and striding away before he could touch me.

That bastard needed to learn how to keep his hands to himself.

AS OUR GROUP walked back to our shelter, the guys chatted around me like they hadn't just voted someone off.

I forced myself to focus on Cameron's plan, and how I'd need to act to make it happen.

I'd thoroughly convinced them that I trusted Julian, or at least trusted him more than I did anyone else. By voting out the person I'd been leaning on, they had basically betrayed me.

They'd taken him out on purpose because of our "connection", so I needed to be upset by that.

I could do upset.

I stayed silent the whole way back, walking away from anyone who fell into step beside me. The remaining eleven guys sat around the fire when we made it back, Cam stoking it higher with his magic. Kyle threw more logs on it, then strode over to me.

I side-stepped his arm when he tried to drape it over my shoulder.

"Come on, Dolly," he teased.

The bastard seemed to think he was being playful, but it just made me want to strangle the guy. I didn't even really like being called *Lolli*, so *Dolly*?

Hard pass.

"Fuck off," I shot back. "You all voted Julian out just because you knew I was starting to trust him."

Kyle spread his hands out. "It's the name of the game, Doll."

"This isn't a game to me. It's my life. My *future*."

"You're making it out of this alive no matter what. The rest of us risk death if we walk away alone, so excuse me for not being empathetic," Kyle drawled.

"I need some air. Don't follow me," I snapped, storming away.

"Moron," someone muttered behind me. I was pretty sure it was Chris.

He'd better have been talking about Kyle.

Even if he wasn't, I wasn't going to mate with him. There had to be a better option.

Cam would make it to the end—he had to, because I wasn't going to tie myself to any of those other bastards at the rate things were going.

CAMERON

I WAITED until a few other guys went off to strategize with their buddies before slipping away. I'd seen the direction Molly was headed, and knew she'd be on her way to our chunk of the beach.

It was a small section, and surrounded by trees that made it difficult for anyone to sneak up on us. I'd hear them coming, the same way I had the night before.

Sure enough, I found her on the sand. Her knees were to her chest, and her eyes were on the ocean.

I sat down beside her, and she didn't waste a moment.

"Julian spoke into my mind after he got voted out," she said, turning to look at me. Those warm, gorgeous brown eyes of hers were slightly concerned. "He said 'well-played'. Do you think he realized what we're doing? What if he told someone else?"

"Julian keeps to himself," I said. "He figured out our plan when I voted for him, and asked me about it during the council. I told him the truth, and he was amused. He wouldn't risk interfering with our game. That would prevent him from playing next time. Our secret is safe."

Molly let out a long breath and nodded. Her shoulders sagged, and I itched to put an arm around her.

I couldn't make a move until she gave me permission, though. She had seemed uncertain about working with me the night before, and I wasn't risking pissing her off again before I knew she was on my side.

I'd win even if she wasn't, of course.

I wasn't walking off the island until she was permanently mine.

But I did want her to make that decision herself, too.

"Who are we going after next?" she asked.

"Reid, Colt, and Kaden. Everyone has started forming alliances, and those three mentioned having suspicions about me. We need them out."

"Before Ev? I thought he was the biggest risk because of the telepathy."

"He could become a risk," I admitted. "But Kaden is well-connected. If he starts spreading suspicions about me and you, the game could be over before it begins."

She took in a long breath and nodded. "I'll start acting like

I'm gravitating toward him. I have to be pissed about the Julian thing for a little longer, though."

"I agree. You played that well, by the way."

"Thanks." She gave me a small smile. "I'm tired of all this shit already. I just want to be done with it."

"We're nowhere near done, Loll."

"I know." She looked back out at the ocean and whispered, "What if our plan fails and I end up having to choose between three pieces of shit? What if I get stuck with *Kyle*? What if—"

"You're not getting stuck with anyone but me." My voice was low, but firm. "If there's ever a sign that I'm going to get voted out, I'll tell you which of the men I trust. You'll pick one of them."

Considering pairing her off with one of the other bastards made me want to burn our island to the fucking ground, but she needed that promise.

And if I couldn't have her, there wasn't a chance in hell I'd put her in the arms of anyone like Kyle.

"How do I even know I can trust you?"

"Look at me, Lolli."

She turned her head, hitting me with those gorgeous eyes again. There was something in them I'd never seen before. Something vulnerable.

"I've never lied to you. I've never manipulated you. The secrets I kept from you were the ones I had to keep to get me here with you, right now."

She swallowed roughly, but nodded. "I'm just... scared, I guess." When she looked back out at the water, the urge to have her on my lap and in my arms again hit me hard.

"Ask me something so I have an excuse to bargain for another hug," I said.

A soft laugh escaped her.

It eased the tension in my chest and the need to have her close.

"What's a peryton? One of the guys said earth elementals can transform into them."

I lifted her off the sand and set her on my lap, turning her so her chest pressed against mine. Her arms went around me, and she held me almost as tightly as I held her.

"They're a mixture between a stag and a large bird. The fae with the brown, furry wings are perytons. Kaden is the only one here."

"Ohh. It's deer fur?"

"Yup."

"Wow. What about griffins? I think they're some kind of bird, but I don't know the details about them either."

"A griffin is a combination of a lion and an eagle. Chris is the only one here. Many of them have white, feathered wings, but some are beige or brown."

"And phoenixes?"

"Flaming golden birds. We're quite beautiful," I said, just to make her smile.

She snorted, and my lips curved upward.

Goal achieved.

"I do like the golden wings. Are your feathers soft?"

"You tell me."

She reached a hand toward my wing, and my abdomen tensed.

"I should warn you, touching a fae's wings is considered intimate," I said, before her fingers brushed me. She deserved the warning, as much as I wanted her to do it.

Her hand paused where it was. "How intimate?"

"What do you want me to compare it to?"

"Is it like a kiss? Or a blow job? Or just touching your cock? Or—"

"The last one." My voice was strained.

I didn't need her help imagining us doing any of those things, but she'd officially given it. I wouldn't be able to get the mental image of her on her knees in front of me out of my head for weeks.

"Could be worse." Her fingers finally brushed my feathers, and my cock throbbed beneath her. There was no doubt she'd felt the hardness already, but I couldn't imagine her ignoring it after that. "Wow, they're really soft. Do the other guys' wings feel like this?"

"I've never asked to touch. You won't either, unless you want to watch me kill someone."

She rolled her eyes, pulling her hand away. "Since when do you get jealous?"

"Since I spent four years making you breakfast and doing absolutely everything with you, Loll. You're mine, remember?"

"I remember you *telling* me that."

"Because it's true." My arms tightened slightly around her back. I needed to let her go and make my way to the shelter again, but I didn't want to.

"How will I know if any of the other guys with mental magic use it against me? No one told me what to look out for."

That was my error.

I needed to stop getting distracted by her body. Winning the game was what mattered. I'd have an eternity with her afterward.

"Telepaths can read minds and speak into them as well. Most humans can't sense when one is in their head, but because you're compatible with us, you have enough magic in your veins to feel the discomfort of their intrusion. You'd notice immediately. Ev is the only telepath left."

She nodded.

I smoothed a hand over her mostly-bare back, needing to touch more of her skin. Knowing that she'd be going to the shelter and lying beside some other fae bastard was enough to make my temper rise.

"Those with dream magic can sway your dreams. You'll wake up feeling like the dreams you experienced were not yours if their magic has touched you. Oren is the only one here with dream magic."

"There's something creepy about that guy," she admitted.

"He's not known for stability. If he ever makes you feel uncomfortable, go to Rhett's side and stay there. I'll deal with him however I have to, should the need arise."

She nodded against me.

"Illusionists can alter how things smell, look, or feel. You'd be able to see through their magic if it was used against you. Knowing it's a possibility prevents you from truly being affected by it."

"Are there any illusionists here?"

"Reid and Colt," I confirmed.

"Alright. Is that the last kind?"

"There's one more. Compulsives. Their magic is the hardest to fight," I admitted. "Even for a compatible mate. Travis is the only compulsive here, other than Rhett. If you find yourself drawn to him in any way, let me and Rhett know immediately."

"If he's that much of a threat, why aren't we going after
him?"

"Because I trust him for the most part. He's also not the
brightest crayon in the box. And he's close allies with Kyle,
who I'm currently working with."

She jerked her body away from mine, though she remained
on my lap. "You're allied with *Kyle*? What the hell, Cam?"

"He suggested an alliance between men you clearly don't
like. I was at the top of his list, and turning him down
would be a terrible idea. He'll take the heat for decisions
about who to vote out, while I'm making the calls. Travis is
a number for us."

"So you're working with the biggest assholes in the game,"
she said flatly.

"The biggest assholes in the game consider me one of
them," I tossed back. "You made me out to be the bad guy
on day one, remember?"

She huffed. "I was pissed at you, for good reason."

"I didn't say you weren't. And that *was* the plan. Right now,
no one sees me or Kyle as threats. That makes them want to
work with us. I have to take advantage of that, and of him,
for as long as possible."

She didn't look happy about it, but she finally nodded. "Fine, I get it. I *really* don't like him, though. He makes me uncomfortable."

"If he ever does something inappropriate, he'll be gone in a heartbeat," I said, my voice even.

It was the truth.

If the bastard did something to my girl, he'd be lucky if I let him live at all. Until then, he was my best shot at winning the game.

"Okay," she agreed. "We should probably go back before anyone gets suspicious."

"I'll head out first and do my best to make it seem like I've been there all along. Stay here another fifteen minutes, and I'll make sure someone gets the idea that we need to send someone to invite you back to camp."

"How are you going to do that without mind magic?" she asked, skeptical.

I winked. "I've got my ways."

She rolled her eyes, but looked much more confident in our plan when I burned my scent off her skin and set her back down on the sand.

I erased my scent from the sand too, just to be safe.

Then, though it was last thing I wanted to do, I slipped back into the jungle and headed toward the lions' den.

MOLLY

SURE ENOUGH, Kaden showed up ten minutes later to invite me back to our shelter.

"It's getting cold out here," he said, his hands in the pockets of his jeans.

It *was* getting cold out there.

I'd been freezing my tits off ever since Cam left with his delicious body heat.

"Fine," I said, standing up and brushing sand off my ass. There was no getting rid of the sand entirely. It was going to be stuck to my skin until I finally got off the island.

"Voting Julian off wasn't personal," Kaden explained. "We know you were sticking with him, but he's well-known in the Society for being quiet and strategic. None of us wanted to risk competing with him as the game progressed."

"I don't want to talk about that," I said flatly.

We walked in silence for a minute before he finally said, "I can give you more information, if that would help you feel better."

I eyed him.

He definitely had my attention.

When he started to walk slower, I did too.

"Cameron has the same reputation as Julian. I'm sure someone's told you that."

"No one tells me anything, actually."

"Not even Cameron?"

"We didn't talk about our personal lives when he was guarding me. We definitely haven't since landing on the island."

He studied me, as if trying to decide if I was telling the truth.

I was.

We *didn't* talk about our lives while he was guarding me, and we still hadn't talked about our pasts. Which was concerning, since I was working with him, but there was no real way around it at the moment.

"If you're that worried about him scheming, just vote him off. I'd be more comfortable with Cameron gone anyway," I said.

It wasn't really a lie.

I *would* be more comfortable with Cameron gone... but not for the reasons he would think.

I'd be more comfortable because I wouldn't have to over-think our hugs on the beach or the fact that I was helping him with his plan to win me like I was a damn prize.

"There are bigger threats," Kaden finally said, still walking slowly. "Not to the game, but to you. Oren is a wildcard. He can be dangerous. And the only way to prove if he's using magic against you is to have your mind read by a telepath, which could interrupt the whole game. Travis is almost as bad."

"What could they do to me?" I wrapped my arms around my middle like I was hugging myself. Mostly because I was cold, but also because I wanted him to think I was clueless and shrinking.

"Oren could plant dreams in your mind. They could be anything from sex dreams to dreams of conversations between you two that make you feel like you can trust him. Travis could manipulate you, making you do things you wouldn't otherwise do."

"How do I protect myself from them?"

"You don't." Kaden's words were apologetic.

"Can I..." I trailed off, like I was rethinking my question.

I really hoped he couldn't tell that I was playing him a little. I didn't have much experience lying. Cameron and I had spent years trading sarcastic responses, so I hoped that had somehow helped my lacking acting skills.

But if Kaden possessed even a sliver of the protective instincts Cameron had, my little idea was going to be a huge success.

"Can you what?"

"Never mind. I don't want to make you a target like Julian," I said quickly.

"I have allies," Kaden urged. "We can protect you. What's the question?"

I hesitated for another minute before finally sighing. "Can I sleep next to you and your friends in the shelter? I hate being close to Kyle, and I don't want to end up next to Oren or Travis if they can manipulate my mind."

"Of course. We'll switch places every night so no one gets particularly suspicious of any of us," Kaden agreed readily. "We'll do what we can to keep you safe from them."

"Thank you."

"Of course." He gave me a small smile, and I tried to return it.

My failed smile only supported the game I was playing.

THE NEXT TWO days felt endless.

It was just me, the guys, and the island.

We ate an assload of fish.

My stomach still rumbled frequently.

We wove more palm fronds and kept beefing up the shelter, finally making it big enough for everyone who wanted to sleep beneath it.

Travis, the guy with the compulsion magic, refused to sleep snuggled up with the other guys. Cam played along with that too, so they both made their own little shelters just out of everyone's sight.

I didn't talk to him the third or fourth day on the island. I couldn't get away without making it obvious. He couldn't either.

So, I stuck with Kaden's trio and otherwise kept to myself. Everyone knew I "felt betrayed" after the Julian vote, so the lack of friendliness seemed natural.

Halfway through the fifth day, a boat showed up to pick us up. The ride was quiet, and we eventually landed on a small, desert island.

I looked up and down the structure that had been built on it, my eyes widening as I realized what the tall, wooden walls and other strange shapes were.

A maze.

A *gigantic* maze.

The sound of mechanisms whirring and the sight of shapes moving overhead told me that the walls of it must've been able to move or rotate or something.

Cameron whistled from where he stood a few guys back from me.

Chris muttered a curse.

Rhett grabbed a sheet of instructions off a wooden bench to the side of the maze. I walked to the bench, assuming it was for me, and sat down as he cleared his throat.

"Today's challenge is simple. Get through the maze. The last two guys through lose their votes in tonight's council. The first two spend the rest of the day and tonight on a private beach with Molly. There will be shade, sustenance, and a bed big enough to share."

My eyes widened.

What if the two guys on the island with me were Kyle and Travis? Or Oren? Or what if they were Cameron's allies, and he got voted out while I wasn't there to see him or act like I was all over Kaden? Or—

"No destroying walls. No magic. No wings. Anyone who breaks any rule or any part of the maze will immediately lose their vote and be removed from the challenge. Are we clear?" Rhett looked out at the group.

All of the men nodded, their wings shimmering for a moment before they disappeared. The men shrank back to their human sizes, their horns vanishing as well.

"There's one final advantage up for grabs," Rhett added. "Somewhere in the maze, there's a box that holds Molly's luxury item. Whoever finds it gets to give it to her, regardless of what place they take in the challenge."

A few eyes gleamed.

Rhett had them all line up at a few different entrances, and then, they began.

He took a seat beside me as everyone disappeared into the maze.

"What's my luxury item?" I asked. "No one told me to pack anything."

"I don't know. It wasn't on any information I received. How are you doing?" He changed the subject, but I didn't mind that.

I was a little surprised he wanted to chat, though. He rarely said a word.

"About as well as I was doing when you threw me out of that airplane."

He chuckled. "Have you felt any mental magic being used against you? If you do, you need to report it to me right away. We have a mated telepath without connections to anyone in the group who will find the truth if you suspect anyone."

I shook my head. "I don't think so. I'll keep that in mind, though."

Rhett nodded.

"You're coming to the private island with me tonight, right?" I asked.

"Of course."

The admission eased my tension just a little.

"And I won't get to return for the voting?"

He shook his head. "The Society wants it to be clear that you're not a part of the game. You're just the final judge."

"I'm just the prize, you mean?" I tossed back.

He didn't answer that one. "This game wasn't my idea, for the record."

"Somehow, that doesn't make my position any better."

He fell silent, so I did too.

We heard curses and shouts a few times as the maze went on. My eyes followed the cameras in the sky above it, all of which followed a different man. They were made in a way that they were hidden for the most part, but when I looked closely, I could see their outlines despite the magic hiding them.

It must've been a complicated maze, because thirty minutes had gone by when the first guy finally burst through.

My stomach clenched when I saw Kyle.

The bastard whooped and did a victory dance before he jogged over and lifted me off the bench. I grabbed him by the hair before he could toss me in the air, and when I hissed at him to put me down, he reluctantly obliged.

I tugged my bikini's tiny strip of fabric back into place (luckily it had only moved a little, so my boob hadn't fallen out or anything) and waited for the next guy to come through.

A few more minutes went by before he emerged.

Oren.

My throat swelled.

He didn't do a victory dance, but high-fived Kyle and grinned at me when he made it out.

My stomach shriveled a little.

The rest of the guys came funneling out over the next hour. No one was bleeding, for once. Cameron was in the middle of the pack, just like he had been in the first challenge.

The last two guys to finish were Kaden and Chris. Chris came out empty-handed, but Kaden was grinning broadly. He had a backpack slung over his shoulder, which I assumed held my luxury item.

The two of them would be losing their votes, so if all went according to plan, Cam would make sure Kaden was gone before he could give me whatever was in the backpack.

I feigned looking out at all the guys as I watched Cameron, hoping for some kind of sign that he was confident everything would be fine even after I left.

He winked at me, and breathing became the tiniest bit easier.

I was led to another boat, with Kyle in front of me and Oren behind me. Though I didn't want to go, I had no choice, so I kept moving.

The boat was tiny, so both guys were squished onto the bench next to me. Both of them pressed up against me, so I tried to make myself smaller, but failed.

When we were finally let off the boat at the island retreat, I let out a long breath and prepared myself for the most uncomfortable hours of my life.

SURPRISINGLY, it wasn't as bad as I'd expected. There was a feast of fruit and burgers, so that was heavenly.

And without so many extra guys around, Kyle eased up on the touchy-feely thing. He gave me space, and Oren did too.

Though Oren still kind of gave me the creeps, he seemed friendlier and more normal without so many men around to compete with.

That was nice.

I still wouldn't have chosen to be there if I had options, but it could've been so much worse.

Nighttime wasn't even awkward. I expected to be beyond uncomfortable, but the guys politely offered to let me sleep on the edge of the bed. They ended up smashed together, and while one of their sides was pressed up against mine, I could almost imagine I was sleeping in the bed alone.

The blanket was amazing, too.

Despite my worry for Cameron, I slept like a rock for the first half of the night.

But somewhere around the middle, I started feeling... different.

My body was flushed when I woke up. I couldn't remember what I'd been dreaming about, but I was slick between my thighs.

That was uncomfortable.

I looked at both guys, but they *looked* like they were sleeping.

So maybe something about falling asleep in a bed with gigantic men made me horny?

I'd never been interested in the reverse-harem thing before, so I wasn't entirely convinced. But what other option was there?

I managed to fall back asleep after a while, but when the dreams came back, they came back insanely intense.

The dreams were *powerful*, and changed rapidly.

Kyle had his hands between my thighs.

Chris was fucking me against a tree.

Oren ate me out with enthusiasm.

Ev's hands were in my hair as I gave him a blowjob.

Reid gripped my ass while I rode his cock.

Kaden held my wrists behind my back while he took me from behind.

It took what felt like ages before I finally managed to wrench myself out of the dreams.

Stumbling from bed, I grabbed the tree I nearly crashed into and held on for dear life. My chest rose and fell rapidly, almost *painfully*.

Those dreams hadn't been mine, had they?

I wasn't normally horny.

I barely even *liked* sex.

It had been almost five years since I'd gone home with someone, and I hadn't even wanted to since.

Oren must've put those dreams in my mind.

...Right?

But the more I looked at him, the more certain I was that he was still sleeping.

My legs shook.

I was drenched between my thighs, but I obviously couldn't do anything about it.

Rhett was relaxing in his chair nearby, watching me closely. He mouthed something that looked like, "You good?"

I gave him a thumbs-up.

Somehow, I must've been the one coming up with all those dreams.

So, I made my way to the beach on shaky legs and sat down in the water, hoping the salt would wash away the scent of my need before the guys woke up and realized what had happened.

MY LEGS WERE steady when the boat returned to the shore with the sunrise, but I kept quiet and didn't say much.

The more I'd thought about it, the more uncertain I was.

I never had sex dreams. I'd never even been attracted to any of the men on the island with me except Cam. And I was only a *little* attracted to him.

Fine, that was a lie.

I was very attracted to him.

The other guys, though? No.

So, the dreams probably weren't mine.

But I couldn't accuse Oren of putting them in my head while he was sleeping. So where did that leave me?

It left me needing to talk to Cameron.

And information he might know.

And... maybe another hug too.

Maybe.

It didn't occur to me that he might not be on the island until we started approaching it.

My entire abdomen clenched at the thought.

When I saw him at the back of the group of men as the boat stopped, I let out a breath I hadn't realized I was holding.

Kyle didn't seem to notice, though Oren gave me a curious look when he heard.

I quickly scanned the group, trying to determine who was gone. None of the guys had their wings or horns out again, so it was a little more challenging to come up with their names. But mentally, I went through the list until I landed on the one who was missing.

Colt.

Kaden was still there, and still holding on to the backpack on his shoulder. My luxury item, whatever it was.

We got off the island, and Kaden immediately pulled me to his side, putting his arm over my shoulder. Though I wanted to cringe away from his touch, he was our next target.

So I couldn't step away.

He steered me away from everyone else, and Reid stepped up to his side as they explained to me in frustration that the other guys had targeted his ally.

"It's my fault," I said quietly. "I got too close to you guys."

"It's not," Kaden argued.

Reid gave him a look that said it was.

"But we're going to have to distance ourselves from you for

now. Hopefully it will buy us enough time to make a few more allies," Kaden added reluctantly.

I sighed. "I get it."

He pulled the backpack from his back. "Here. I got this for you."

I accepted it and undid the zipper. When I opened it and found a huge, soft orange blanket I recognized from my living room, my eyes burned a little.

I was so tired, and so uncertain about everything. I just needed to talk to Cam, but I had no way of doing that without making someone suspicious.

Zipping it back up, I blinked away the tears I wouldn't let fall. "Thank you. This means a lot to me."

With that, I stepped back up to the rest of the guys and cleared my throat. Most of them were already looking at me, so it wasn't a stretch to get everyone else's attention.

My eyes were still a tiny bit watery, and I noticed concern on a few men's faces. "I need some space," I said to them. "From all of you. Just... leave me alone for a while."

With that, I walked away.

I wouldn't go to mine and Cam's section of the beach. They'd notice if he slipped away.

But I did go as far down our beach as I possibly could before I tucked myself up against a rock and closed my eyes, trying to decide what the hell I was going to do.

seven

MOLLY

THE GUYS LEFT me alone for around half an hour before I heard footsteps on the sand.

My stomach tensed.

The intruder sat down beside me, leaving a solid two-foot gap, and my body relaxed slightly when I caught a whiff of Cameron's scent.

He always smelled good.

How had I never noticed that before?

"What happened on the island, Loll?" Cam cut right to the chase.

"You shouldn't be here. People will see you."

I wiped at a tear that escaped.

Dammit, I wasn't supposed to cry.

"The guys all voted me over here since I'm the one you hate who isn't always touching you. It was between me and Kyle. They weren't about to send someone you might actually hug."

A teary laugh escaped me.

"Shh. Try not to look like you're having fun," he whispered.

"They can't even see me. I'm hidden behind a rock."

"I know. They can see me, though."

I nodded.

"What happened?" He cut to the chase again.

My face burned. "I don't know."

"Molly," he warned.

When he pulled out my actual name, I knew he wasn't joking around anymore.

"I had sex dreams," I whispered. "I never have sex dreams."

"About Oren?" The words were growled.

"About multiple different guys here. I thought it might've been because of him, but he was sleeping. So it couldn't have been his magic, right? Maybe I'm just tired, or losing my mind, or—"

"Fae always look like they're sleeping when they're using dream magic," Cameron said sharply. "Did you tell Rhett?"

"No. I wasn't going to get him involved if I was just horny for the first time in forever."

Cam leaned closer to me, his eyes flooded with something I'd never seen before. It almost looked like... violence.

"Oren attacked you when he put those dreams in your head. I should've warned you what it would look like when he did, and I'm sorry for that. Would you like to be the one to inform Rhett, or should I?" His voice was calm.

Too calm.

There was no teasing and no sarcasm, for once.

"I should probably do it," I whispered. "I just don't want to."

"I would be thrilled to handle this, Lolli."

As much as I wanted to be the kick-ass woman who dealt with that shit herself, his offer felt like a weight off my shoulders.

I could do it... but he could too.

And if he wanted to, I didn't think it would hurt to let him. It would just make things slightly easier for me.

So I nodded.

He took my hand, squeezed it, then strode across the sand.

I peered over the rock to watch him go.

My eyes widened when his wings emerged from his back, his horns growing on his head as he shifted forms.

I gasped when he burst into flames before swinging his fist at Oren's face.

Hard.

Blood, curses, and magic spewed.

A solid thirty seconds of shock passed before the other guys ripped them away from each other.

I was far enough away that I couldn't hear what Cameron spat at a few of the guys—but I did hear the resulting snarls.

All hell broke loose for two minutes before Rhett looked at me. His expression was dark.

I resisted the urge to duck behind my rock again.

Shook my head instead.

Rhett grabbed Oren from the pile of attackers, ignoring the blood dripping from multiple wounds, and shoved him up against a tree.

I stayed where I was as a few of the men crossed the beach, heading toward me. Cameron wasn't one of them.

"Rhett sent for a telepath to validate the claim," Kyle growled, remaining beside the other men. "He'll be here within ten minutes, and he'll need to talk to you."

I stood.

None of them tried to touch me or move closer to me.

"We'll kill him ourselves when we get permission," Chris said.

All of them looked pissed.

And while that probably should've scared me, it actually made me feel a little bit better.

THE CONVERSATION with the telepath was short. He pulled the truth from my mind quickly, confirming that Oren had, in fact, invaded my dreams.

He was supposed to force Oren off the island with him, but Oren was dead so fast he didn't get the chance.

I wasn't *positive* which of the men killed him, but the burns on his skin told me I knew.

All of the guys were angry that the rules had been broken, but none of them were anywhere near as protective of me as Cam.

EVERYONE GAVE me space for the rest of the day.

When night came around, Travis kindly offered to give me his shelter away from the rest of the men. I thanked him and accepted, since I had a blanket to stay warm after the last challenge.

Hidden just out of their sight, I stayed awake until the last of them was asleep.

Cameron did too.

When it had been silent for long enough, Cam finally left his own shelter, stepping into my view and tilting his head toward our beach.

He disappeared, but I knew he'd be walking there alone just to buy us a little more security.

When I reached the sand, his arms went around me so fast, I sucked in a breath as he crushed me to his chest. After a moment's surprise, mine went around him too, and I hugged him back almost as tightly as he held me.

"I'm so fucking sorry, Loll." His words were muffled against my ear. Muffled, and angry. "I should never have let that happen."

"There was nothing you could do."

"I could've been out of that maze in ten minutes flat," he growled back. "I should've been on that island with you. I should've been watching that bastard and keeping you safe. I should've—"

"You're holding back so you don't look like a threat," I interrupted. "Right?"

"Of course I am. I'm not leaving this game without your soul tied to mine."

"If you were on that island with me, you could've been voted out the next time. You had to be here. I need you with me at the end so I don't have to marry a stranger, Cam." My voice shook a little.

"I know, Loll."

"So stop blaming yourself. It happened, but it's over. I'm okay."

"You've been pale and quiet all day. You're not okay."

I let out a long breath and shook my head against his chest. "I'm not... I don't know. It was just... I've never liked sex. I'm just confused."

Cam squeezed me, then eased us both to the sand. I ended up on his lap again, like I had the last two times we met there, but it felt different.

More comfortable.

More intimate, maybe.

"I heard you use your vibrator in the shower a few times a week, Lollipop. You like sex," he said, his eyes meeting mine.

It should've felt weird to be sitting on Cam's lap. And talking about that, with *him* of all people. We'd been enemies. Or at least rivals.

Or maybe just friends who liked to argue. I wasn't sure what to call us anymore.

But it didn't feel weird.

It felt safe.

And right.

"I like *orgasms*," I corrected.

"You do know that sex is a way to have orgasms with another person, right?"

I rolled my eyes. "I know that's the theory, but it doesn't really work like that. Never did for me, at least."

"You didn't have the right partner, then."

"You're not wrong about that. I guess I convinced myself that there was no right partner. And the dreams just… surprised me."

"Did you dream about me?" His gaze was curious, in a dark way that made me a little warm.

"No."

"Did you want to?"

"I would've preferred it over dreaming about them."

He tapped my temple. "I don't like knowing you have mental images of the other men on this island fucking you. I *really* don't like knowing you don't have one of me in there too."

"Don't you?" I drawled.

"No. And I'm tempted to do something about that, Lolli."

"Like what?"

"Like slip my hand into these ridiculously small shorts and play with your clit until I get to watch you come on my lap."

My cheeks flushed.

Wetness gathered between my thighs.

"Doesn't exactly sound sexy," I lied.

"Maybe you'd have more fun if I set you down on this rock, stripped you bare, and buried my face between those pretty little thighs so I could taste your pleasure." His thumb dragged slowly over my hip.

I arched against his erection, just a little bit. Neither of us had ever mentioned it, but his desire for me had been clear every time we were on the beach like that.

"Still not very convincing," I said, my chest rising and falling a little faster.

He leaned his head down until his lips brushed the shell of my ear. I tilted to the side a little, giving him more access, and he lifted a hand to the back of my neck. His thumb brushed the side of it lightly, making me shiver.

"You'd rather I just cut this tiny bikini off your body and fuck you hard on this sand until we come together, wouldn't you, Lollipop? You want my release inside you, telling every man on this island that you're mine."

I was breathing so fast I was panting.

My breasts pressed hard against his chest with every rough inhale.

He undid the button on my shorts with one hand, easing them down my thighs. They'd gotten looser with every day we survived on nothing but fish.

When they hit the sand, he opened my thighs wider and set me up over the erection straining against his shorts.

I took an unsteady breath in at the delicious pressure of him.

My eyes fluttered closed.

My head tipped back.

His teeth caught my earlobe and tugged lightly.

"Use me, Lolli," he murmured.

It was the sexiest thing anyone had ever said to me.

My hips moved slowly, then faster, as I ground myself against him. He kneaded my ass slowly as I got myself closer and closer to the edge.

His cock felt huge, and his heat made me want more of him pressed against me.

Not just *against* me, either.

I wanted him *inside* me.

Filling me.

Making me his.

Bringing him pleasure too.

Making me hot in every way there was, as—

He pressed his lips to mine, swallowing my cries of pleasure as I found the release I'd been seeking. My channel clenched around nothing, but the climax was still fierce.

He dragged his tongue over my top lip before he let my mouth go. "You're fucking gorgeous."

I leaned against him, my forehead on his cheek as I pressed my chest to his just a little tighter. "That was so good."

"Better than your vibrator, huh?"

"Way better."

"You love sex, Lollipop. Or at least, you'll love it with me."

Goosebumps broke out on my skin. "Maybe."

He chuckled. "You'll see. The next time you want me to sneak out here with you, just give me the nod after everyone's asleep."

Cameron grabbed my shorts, turned me around on his lap, and tugged them back up my legs.

"I can get myself dressed," I said, still just a little dazed.

"I know you can." He abandoned the shorts halfway up my thighs. My body clenched when his long, strong fingers slipped into the front of my bikini bottoms and slowly freed the fabric from my folds.

When he was done, he finished pulling my shorts up and buttoned them back in place.

He lifted his finger to his lips and sucked lightly to clean it. His chest rumbled against my back, and I fought to ignore the desire that was pooling between my legs once again.

"After you're mine," he murmured, lips brushing my ear again. "I'll be able to make you come with my fire."

"How?"

"When you choose me, you'll find out." He kissed my cheek. "I'm going to have to burn the scent of pleasure off your skin. Need me to get you off again first?"

My face flushed. "No, I don't *need* another climax."

"Good. I don't think I could let you put these clothes on again if I took them off right now."

"They barely count as clothes. Everyone in the world is seeing pretty much my whole bod..." I trailed off, my gaze lifting to the sky.

Sure enough, there were cameras trained on us. Hidden cameras, but seeing through their camouflage had become easy for me.

"Shit," I whispered. "We totally just made a porno."

Cam snorted. "Neither of us was naked."

"Still."

"When I fuck you on this beach, I'll make sure to keep us covered with my wings," he said, his voice playful again.

"That's never going to happen," I tossed back.

"Whatever you say, Lollipop." He sucked lightly on my shoulder before his fire raced up and down my skin. "We better take a dip in the ocean just to make sure I erased the scent entirely."

I nodded.

"You're aware that you're not letting any other male on this island touch you like I just did, right?" he asked.

I rolled my eyes at him, but confirmed.

We headed down to the water hand-in-hand before making our way back to the shelters separately.

Even biting my lip, I couldn't wipe my smile off my face the whole way back.

MOLLY

THE NEXT THREE DAYS WERE... odd.

The men gave me more space than before, which was appreciated, but they started looking at me differently.

Like they didn't just want me as a mate, but *wanted me*, wanted me.

Kyle, Ev, and Reid all started walking around absolutely naked. When I asked them why they'd stripped down, training my eyes on their faces, they lied about wanting to be comfortable.

Cameron had a stupidly attractive smirk on his face every single day. I itched to ask him why he was so happy, but couldn't sneak away long enough to meet up with him.

The other guys were staying up as late as I did.

They'd sprawl out beside the fire and stare at me.

It was unnerving.

Though I had a feeling that something was going on without me realizing it, there was nothing I could do about it, so I tried to ignore the staring and the attempts at nude seduction or whatever. No one was touching me or trying to talk me into anything, so it wasn't really *bothering* me.

And hey, the guys *were* nice to look at.

ON DAY EIGHT, there was no vote. Oren had taken care of that for us. The men participated in a mud race instead, which ended with me on yet another date with Kyle.

He still didn't put pants on, despite the mud in places that had likely never seen sun before.

We ate steak together on an empty beach, and I finally asked him the question that had been on my mind for days.

"Why are all of you acting weird? It wasn't like this when we first got here. Everyone was wearing pants. And don't give me some bullshit about comfort."

I didn't gesture to his junk.

It seemed unnecessary.

"Oh, that. We can smell your pheromones."

"My *what-a-mones*?"

"Your pheromones." Kyle cut a gigantic chunk of steak and popped it in his mouth. "When a compatible mate starts actively wanting someone to share her bed, her scent changes as her pheromones activate. Male fae within a hundred miles can smell it. That's how we used to find mates before the game shows started."

He spoke with food in his mouth, but by the grace of whatever insane genetics he had, still managed not to be revolting as he did.

My eyes narrowed. "You're telling me you guys started walking around naked because you think I'm *horny*?"

"Horny for a mate." He ruffled his hair. "I'm here and willing, by the way, should you ever need to scratch an itch."

"Oh, screw off," I grumbled, leaning back in my chair. As tired as I was of fish, I didn't think I could eat anymore steak. My stomach was too twisted.

The pheromones weren't wrong.

I *was* horny.

Not for a mate, but for Cam.

Who wanted me as his mate.

So...

Dammit.

I had been thinking about our tryst on the beach way too often. Maybe if I could stop thinking about it, and about him, I could get the pheromones to go away.

"Would the smell fade if I hooked up with someone?" I asked.

Kyle snorted. "Only if it was bad. And fae are *very* good at sex."

Yeah, I'd realized that.

Cam and I hadn't even taken our clothes off, and it had still been the best sexual encounter of my life. Not that I had anything good to compare it to.

"So how do I get rid of the pheromones?" I asked.

"Take a mate."

"How do you take a mate?"

"I'm not technically allowed to say until after the show's over. But it's pretty simple. Basically just involves sex and magic."

Was that what Cam was talking about when he mentioned getting me off with his fire?

Because I'd been thinking about that too much, too. Way too much.

Kyle inhaled deeply, his chest rumbling. "Your pheromones just got stronger. You totally want to fuck me."

"No, I don't." I set my fork down, giving up on the rest of my food entirely.

The giant sitting across from me would eat it.

He chuckled, but sure enough, finished both of our plates in record time.

· · ·

THINGS WERE JUST as weird when we made it back to the shelter. Since there were still three more days before another vote, things were more laid-back.

But Harker had stopped wearing pants too.

Yay.

WHEN DAY eleven finally came around, I was long-past ready to boot someone else off the island. A lot of *someones*, I hoped. Every *someone* who wasn't wearing pants, in fact. And a few others too.

I still hadn't managed to get away with Cam, which meant I was stupidly horny.

And probably even more *pheremoney*. Which was not a word, but I was too annoyed to care.

Everyone was watching me like a damn hawk.

After my conversation with Kyle, they all thought I was going to jump into bed with someone, and hoped to be that someone.

THE BOAT RIDE to the challenge that day was far too long. I managed to tuck myself between two guys who weren't in the nude, thankfully. Neither of which was Cameron.

As much as I didn't like that, I still wasn't risking exposing his plan. He'd be off the island ridiculously fast if anyone found out.

And that was the last thing we wanted.

I had tried to talk to Kaden as much as possible, but he was avoiding me for the sake of attempting to stay in the game. I hoped my effort was enough, but wasn't expecting it to work in my favor.

If it didn't, Cam would just have to figure out a way to get Kaden out on his own. I saw him chatting with all the other men often enough that I was hopeful he could manage it.

The challenge was a complex puzzle. The prize was a snorkeling date to a large reef nearby and a meal on the way there.

For once, Kyle didn't win.

Ev did, however. He was the other telepath, which made me a little nervous.

He got to pick another guy to go with us, and surprised me by choosing Jim.

We wouldn't be getting back from the reef until after that night's vote, which made me nervous, but I had to hide those nerves. As far as the guys knew, I wasn't in favor of anyone.

Except possibly Kaden.

The boat they'd provided to take us to the reef was much bigger than the usual speedboat, so there was space for us to get comfortable. I sat on the ledge near the front so I had a good view, my legs dangling off the side. Ev and Jim sat on either side of me.

They were two of the men I knew the least, so I was actually kind of looking forward to talking to them. There was still a chance Cam could get booted, and I would have to choose someone else. In case that did happen, I needed to get to know everyone.

Then again, how well did I even know Cameron?

I didn't know much of anything about his life before guarding me. He'd never told me about his past, or who he was outside his job.

I knew he had a lot of connections, and had somehow used those connections to get himself set up as my guard, but that was it.

Still, I trusted him.

Mostly.

And yeah, I wanted him.

Insanely.

But at the rate things were going, I would know more about Kyle than I did about Cam.

Which made me less than certain about my plan.

I did trust him not to hurt me, though. Which was more than I could say about anyone else on the island, except maybe Rhett.

"Finally, I get a break from Kyle," I drawled, as the ocean's spray tickled my legs.

Jim snorted. "It's a miracle. That asshole's been driving all of us crazy since day one."

I smiled. "You *could* vote him out and save all of us from the suffering."

"We could... but you're not going to pick him," Ev said with a grin. "So he's a safe choice to take to the end."

I rolled my eyes. "Sanity should come before safe choices."

"Survival has to come before sanity," Ev corrected.

I gave a dramatic sigh, and both men chuckled.

"So you're an accountant?" Ev asked me, as the ride continued.

"Yep." I nodded confirmation. "Money became an even bigger problem for humans when the world was moving toward its end, so accounting seemed safe. And I always liked math. It's been steady since you guys stepped in and started all this game show stuff, so I can't complain."

"Do you enjoy it?" Jim asked.

"Yeah. I actually kind of miss my job. They skipped over me every time it came to promotions, because I had to disclose that I was a compatible mate, but I still liked it. I had friends there. Or at least enough acquaintances to have fun at work."

"Do you think you'll want to go back there after the show is over?"

"I don't think *anything* about when the show is over. The Society made it very clear that I have to live wherever my mate wants me to live. I figured I'd be expected to pop out babies and keep the house clean or some shit like that."

Jim made a face. "Sounds like hell."

"To me, yeah." I shot him a curious look. "But why does it sound like that to you?"

"You've got ten ancient fae on this show, Molly. None of us are looking to settle down. We've *been* settled down for far too long, and we want change. Passion. Sex. Fun."

"No one told me that," I said, suddenly unsure about what to expect from the future. "They told me to pack my things because I'd be moving in with my mate after the show ended, whether I liked it or not."

"They probably just needed the apartment for another compatible mate and their guard," Ev said.

I bit my lip.

I hadn't gotten any information about what to expect my life to look like. I hadn't asked any of the fae what they wanted to do with their futures, either. I assumed that because they were unmated, and couldn't reproduce without a mate, they would be looking to have lots of babies.

Maybe I was wrong.

Hopefully I was wrong.

"It's very difficult for fae women to get pregnant," Ev added.

"I'm not a fae woman."

"You will be, when you're mated. Your mate's power will become yours as well."

Oh.

Damn.

I hadn't known that, either.

"The Society should really put that information in their welcome handbook," I finally said.

"There's a welcome book?" Jim's eyebrows lifted like he was impressed.

"No. They should make one, though."

The look he gave me said that wasn't going to happen.

Ev gave me an apologetic smile. "I'll see if I can do anything about it after the game's over."

"You have connections in the Society?" I asked.

"Kind of."

"Who are the most connected?"

"Cameron, then Chris. Travis would be a close third. Cam's the only one who knows everyone, though."

He'd told me as much.

"Does having connections make them a risk?" I wondered.

Ev shrugged. "Not really. Knowing you well would be the biggest risk factor, after we've exhausted everyone you show interest in."

My stomach tightened a little.

He was talking about someone in particular, and there was only one person who fit the bill.

"No one here knows me," I said.

"Cameron lived with you. Even if you don't get along, he likely knows your favorite foods. Your favorite movies. The way you dress. How you do your hair. If you get your nails done. The places you like to shop. What treat you buy when you've had a bad day. Where—"

"I get it," I said, interrupting him.

The twist in my stomach was starting to become a knot.

"But I think I've made it pretty clear I have no interest in mating with him. He kept the truth from me for years, and I would never tie myself to someone that comfortable with lying to me."

Ev nodded. "I believe that. But he does have allies. And if he knows you as well as he should after guarding you, he can tell his allies exactly how to win you over, giving any of them the upper hand."

My forehead creased. "That's ridiculous. Knowing what I like to wear isn't an advantage for anyone."

"We'll have to agree to disagree," Ev said casually.

The knot in my stomach remained.

"Maybe we should target Cam next," Jim suggested.

"Let's not talk about the game anymore," Ev said, cutting a look at Jim.

He was totally planning that.

Ev was going to go after Cameron.

The knot in my stomach tightened.

I was going to have to get Cam alone so I could warn him.

The guys spent the rest of the trip telling me about their lives, and I listened as actively as I could. If I didn't play along, they'd realize I was worrying.

And they needed to sincerely believe that I wasn't working with Cameron.

So, I acted like I was enjoying the date while I hoped desperately that Cam would still be on the beach when we got back.

nine

CAMERON

I FOUGHT the urge to tap my foot, sprawled out on the sand beside the fire.

Molly had been gone far too long. Ev and Jim were among the better options for her on the island, which she would likely realize if she spent time with them.

I just didn't want her to realize it.

What if she enjoyed her time with them too much?

What if she realized she'd prefer one of the other bastards on the island?

I wasn't going to walk away from her, regardless of whether someone else charmed her. I'd just have to figure something out.

Kyle plopped down beside me. We'd voted Kaden out an hour earlier, and he would not be missed. He had been the biggest remaining threat to my position in the game, so it was a relief to have him gone.

There were still other threats, of course.

They were just more manageable.

"So, what's our plan?" Kyle asked.

"I thought we'd already figured that out."

Kyle grinned. "Not *that* plan. What's our plan to make one of our asses the winner? In case you haven't noticed, our girl only looks at either of us when she has no other choice."

I bit back my irritation.

She was *my* girl. Not *ours*.

It would be a great day when I could finally get her away from Kyle.

"I haven't thought that far ahead," I lied. "I guess as we get closer to the end, her options will dwindle, and she'll be forced to give us a chance. We just need a third she doesn't like, so the three of us can battle it out when we get there."

Kyle nodded as if that was a reasonable plan.

It was bullshit, but he would learn that when Molly picked me.

He scanned the other guys. A few of them were sleeping in the shelter. Two were tossing a coconut back and forth on the beach. Three were adding more palm fronds and bamboo to Molly's little shelter. That was probably an attempt to win her over by providing comfort.

It wasn't going to work, but I wouldn't stop them. I would make it more comfortable myself if I could do so without causing suspicion.

"Travis is our best bet," Kyle finally decided. "I can talk about how shitty it is to be under compulsion during my next date with her."

I nodded slowly.

The idea was poor, but I couldn't tell him that.

"She might know that her mate can't use his magic on her that way," I said.

"Nah. We'll scare her into thinking he can," Kyle said.

I bit back a snort.

The man was a class act.

I agreed with his shitty plan, then started talking about sports to distract him from the competition.

A few minutes later, Molly's boat arrived.

I resisted the urge to put myself at the front of the group and help her back onto the beach. Making myself a target would only screw my game, though I itched to claim her publicly.

Unlike me, Kyle didn't hesitate. His was the hand that helped her.

It irritated me, but knowing she didn't like him eased that.

It had been too long since I'd gotten her alone. Nearly a week. On the island, that felt like a lifetime. But with everyone's eyes on her, there was no way to do so without putting a target on my back.

The guys in the shelter stumbled out in front of me, and I followed them to the group. We were at the back, but that was the best place for me at the moment.

Molly greeted everyone, taking in the fact that Kaden had been voted out. I expected her to go straight to her shelter, given that it was already late.

Instead, she headed for the campfire.

A few guys exchanged surprised looks.

Someone muttered, "Don't overwhelm her. If we act cool, maybe she'll make a habit of this."

I bit back a snort.

If they tried to manipulate Molly, she'd see straight through them. I hadn't had the chance to tell her every little thing about fae, but she was wickedly smart. She would pick up on their efforts even if she didn't call them out for it.

A few of the guys reluctantly went back to the shelter to give her space.

Kyle followed her right to the fire, of course.

I sprawled out on the sand a ways in front of the two of them, not intervening, but staying close enough that I could hear. She had obviously taken a seat by the fire for a reason.

Ev joined the men in the shelter.

Jim headed for the bathroom.

Kyle asked her about the reef, and she gave him simple answers.

It was beautiful.

The sunset was gorgeous.

The food was good.

After a while, the guys in the shelter started snoring. One first, then a few more.

Molly whispered, barely loud enough for me to hear, "Kyle, can you see if Ev is asleep?"

That caught my interest.

"Sure." Kyle strode over to the shelter, his footsteps loud. He whistled loudly as he went, and when he walked past it, called out, "Sorry, gotta piss."

A groan sounded in the shelter, but it wasn't Ev's.

"You listening, Cam?" Molly murmured. Kyle was far enough that he wouldn't have heard.

I dipped my head in the smallest nod, answering her question in a way that couldn't create suspicion if anyone was watching.

Kyle shuffled back loudly before plopping down beside her again. "He's out."

The man's whispers were so damn loud.

"We were talking on the boat, and Ev told me that you're a threat," Molly said, her voice soft.

Fuck.

Though she was talking to Kyle, I knew her words were for me.

"Bastard," Kyle growled. "Why does he think that?"

"You've been winning so many challenges that he thinks you'll make it to the end easily if he doesn't get rid of you."

That obviously wasn't pointed to me.

I didn't know exactly why he was going after me, and I didn't think Molly would come right out with the answer. Not if it was something that could possibly make Kyle suspicious as well.

"He'll be the next to go," Kyle swore.

"Just be careful. If he realizes you're coming after him, he could retaliate," Molly warned. "And you don't want him trying to convince everyone else that you should be a target."

"I'll keep quiet about it," he agreed, though he had to grit out the words.

I doubted he would.

But I could probably spin it in a way that made it sound like Kyle was pissed just because Ev won a challenge instead of him. He obviously didn't do well with losing.

"Good luck," Molly said quietly. "I'm going to bed. Night."

"Goodnight," Kyle grumbled.

Though I didn't let myself watch her go, I listened to her footsteps, and to the sounds of her shelter creaking as she sat down.

Kyle stormed over to me, glaring down at me. "Change of plans. We're going after Ev."

"Good idea," I said, as if it was all on him.

He grinned wickedly, and when he held out his fist, I bumped mine against it.

He wasn't alert enough to realize what was happening between me and Molly... but he was the perfect ally.

MOLLY

EV GOT VOTED out on day fourteen.

I felt bad for my role in that, but as much as I kind of liked his personality, I didn't know the guy. Keeping him around was too much of a risk.

I didn't know Cam's past, or a whole lot about him, but I did know that he would treat me well.

And that we could have fun together.

Jim went on day seventeen.

Harker was gone on day twenty.

And then, there were five.

The mood on the island grew more serious as the numbers dwindled. Kyle still wasn't wearing pants, but everyone else was.

We were all aware that there were only two more votes before we got down to the final three. And when we got to the final three, it would be *my* game, not theirs.

No one was sleeping much. All of the guys seemed suspicious that I'd sneak away with someone if they closed their eyes for too long, so there were always at least two men awake.

Which meant I hadn't had the chance to be alone with Cameron in ages.

We were still on the same page, I thought.

But I was getting more nervous about how little I knew about him, and the fact that I was going to be *mated* soon.

We would have time to get to know each other a little more when the voting was finally over, but still.

It was a huge decision. One that would determine the rest of my life.

The ride to the challenge on day twenty-four was quiet.

The speedboat was squished, as always, and I still wasn't next to Cameron. Luckily, I'd managed to put myself between Chris and Reid, so Kyle's junk wasn't anywhere near me.

When we landed on the beach of a large, jungle island, my forehead creased.

There were no visible obstacles or events in sight, which seemed concerning. The only time that had happened was on the first day, when the guys hunted for the shitty survival gear.

I took my seat on the bench Rhett gestured me to, and he cleared his throat.

"I'm sure you've all been waiting for this day," he drawled. "Because it's care package day."

Kyle whooped.

Reid whistled.

Travis smiled.

Cam grinned.

Chris did a little dance.

"Today, no one loses," he said. "Everyone goes hunting for their package, and everyone comes out with it. Whoever finds Molly's gets thirty minutes alone with her. Everyone else gets ten. First guy back goes first, and etcetera."

No one had any questions, so they all headed into the jungle.

They did so with far less energy than they had the first day, though.

Rhett sat down next to me. "Only two more votes," he said.

"Seven more days, and I'll be a mated woman," I agreed, trepidation making me a little nauseous.

Or maybe that was all the fish. I hoped to never be the reason another sea creature died after I left the island.

"Each of the guys' bags has an asset folder. This is one of their largest chances to convince you to pick them," Rhett said.

Asset folders.

Lovely.

"The Society is impressed," he added. "They put together the first episode and aired it already, and it was a hit. *Survival* will be a regular after this."

I grimaced. "Yay."

"Most of the men will be coming back for the next season," he said, watching me closely.

"That sucks for them."

"The majority are too close to dying to have any other option."

I bit my lip.

I hadn't thought about that in a while. The dying thing.

If I didn't mate with Cam, what were his chances of surviving?

And if I didn't mate with him, who else would I choose?

Definitely not Kyle. That was a hard pass.

I didn't want Travis, either.

Or Reid.

Or Chris.

Chris was probably my second-best option. He wasn't an ass. He just sort of went with the flow, and obviously picked the right group to ally with from the beginning. I'd never been on a date with him, so he had either been holding back like Cam, or he was just worse than Kyle at all the challenges.

Both of which seemed like possibilities.

Whatever happened, I was pretty much trapped. And I really didn't like knowing that.

"Who won't be coming back if they don't win?" I asked, hoping the question was vague enough. Rhett had seen me with Cameron, so he knew our plan even if we hadn't had the chance to talk about it in a while.

"Just Cam," Rhett said.

I bit down harder on my lip.

The first guy emerged with a bag a few minutes later.

I expected Kyle. He wouldn't care about finding my supposed care package. He just liked to win.

Instead, I got Cam.

He must've wanted privacy when he showed me the package he'd put together, or he wouldn't have let himself get back first.

My eyes widened when he walked out in a very familiar yellow sweatshirt.

He winked at me, and I sat down with him at Rhett's instructions. The spot was tucked away so no one else could see us, but close enough that we were still within Rhett's line of sight.

"Are you kidding me?" I asked, fighting back a smile.

He winked. "Good morning, Sunshine."

I laughed, and he pulled the sweater over his head before handing it to me.

"Where's your asset folder?" I teased.

He grinned and pulled it out of his bag, handing it over. When I opened it, I found pictures of a pretty house that looked over a gorgeous beach.

"There's sand?" I asked.

"I'll keep it off the floors for you."

I made a face, and his grin widened.

Below that, I found a few pictures of the interior of the house, which were all beautiful.

I paused when I found the ones beneath the house pics.

There was a picture of him with my grandma.

One of the coffee shops I frequented.

My favorite grocery store.

My favorite movie.

My favorite couch pillow.

My thermostat, set much lower than it would've been if I were the one paying for it."

I closed the folder and met his gaze.

He handed me a bag of my favorite candy—the same lollipops he'd caught me eating when he walked into my apartment and gave me that nickname.

Then, he put a small box on my lap.

My throat swelled when I realized what it was, but I didn't open it.

"This was supposed to be *your* care package," I said, my voice growing quieter.

The smile on his face was playful, but soft. "I care about you."

"I feel like I barely know you," I admitted. "Yes, I trust you. But you know all these things about me, because you were guarding me. Who are *you*?"

His smile faded, slightly. "That is a very long story. Not one I can tell in the three minutes we have left."

I nodded, though emotions were still gathered in my throat.

Cam packed everything except the asset folder back into the bag, and left it next to me. "Better leave the sweatshirt and ring in there until we get down to the final three."

I nodded again. "Do you think you can do it?"

His lips curved upward. "Hell, yes."

A snort escaped me, and he winked before he stood up and walked away.

Despite my uncertainty, one thing was very clear.

Cameron *did* care about me.

KYLE WAS SECOND.

He dumped everything out of his bag, and showed all of it to me.

A hat with his favorite football team's logo.

A pair of expensive socks.

A picture of him and his sister. That one made me feel kind of bad for not liking him, honestly. He seemed proud of her, and I knew there weren't many female fae. He'd probably been a good, protective older brother. I'd always wanted one of those.

After those three things, he pulled out his asset folder.

He showed me dozens of pictures of his mansion, his pools (yes, pool*s*), and his massive garage full of luxury cars. He gave me bank statements, and a plan for the *monthly allowance* I'd have.

"How do you feel about your mate working?" I asked him.

He laughed. "I'd be ashamed if my female ever had to lift a hand a day of her life. Providing for you is my job."

Oof.

I mean, that was probably *someone's* dream answer.

Just not mine.

"What would I do with all my time, then?" I asked.

He shrugged. "Whatever you want."

"What if I wanted to work?"

"Then you'd find a new hobby, or we could travel or something."

That answer was slightly better.

It just wasn't what I would've hoped for.

Kyle wasn't a horrible guy, but we weren't compatible. If he made it to the end, which seemed likely, I'd have to pick literally anyone other than him.

Luckily, our time was up soon. He put his ballcap on his head, tugged his fancy socks on, and grinned as he left me sitting on the sand with the folder.

I didn't bother glancing up at him.

I'd seen plenty of his junk without getting a glimpse of him wearing nothing but socks.

TRAVIS WAS NEXT.

Like Cam, he brought things for *me* in his care package.

They weren't as personalized, but he didn't know me before, so that was understandable.

There was a massive, melted bar of chocolate.

A thicker, warmer blanket than the one I already had.

And a locket necklace with a picture of his house in it. Apparently, he lived on a private island, in a mansion of his own.

His asset folder had pictures of his home as well as ones of his family. He didn't have a bank account summary sheet, or anything like that, which made me feel like he'd be a better option than Kyle, at least.

REID WAS THE FOURTH GUY, and he proudly showed me photos of the apartment complex he owned and lived in. His penthouse was on the top floor, and had a gorgeous view of a large city I'd never visited before.

His package had a letter for me, written by his mother, trying to persuade me what a perfect mate he'd be. It was accompanied by a family heirloom ring that I quickly handed back. I told him I'd accept it if I chose him on the final day, and he reluctantly agreed.

Afterward, I learned that his parents lived in his penthouse with him.

That was a hard pass.

I was sure they were lovely people, but I wanted privacy.

Chris was the final competitor to return, and he did so with both his bag and my own.

Granted, my bag was one I'd never seen before.

We spent the next half hour laughing over the stupid items the Society had sent for me. I noticed Cam watching us at one point, but didn't think anything of it.

It included a tiny, hot pink bikini that was somehow even smaller than the green one I had on. Also, a box of condoms, and a mesh sunhat that absolutely wouldn't keep any sunshine out of my face.

The Society was made up of assholes.

Ass.

Holes.

But, Chris was decent. He lived on a ranch out in some southern state I'd heard of, but never visited. There was no sand but a lot of dirt, which he warned me about.

Everyone who paid attention knew how I felt about sand.

He had three younger brothers, all of whom were already mated. Two of them had been on *Bachelorette*, and won, but I hadn't watched any part of their seasons.

Despite his big family, Chris was fine with whatever I wanted as far as children went. He didn't care whether or not I worked, and would support me either way.

It seemed like he just wanted a companion, which I could understand. I hadn't spent much time alone, given that

Cam had been guarding me 24/7, but having no one on your side felt like shit. It had been me against the Society ever since I got my bloodwork back. And Cam had always seemed like part of the Society, given his job.

So... that was something to think about.

There were a *lot* of somethings to think about.

At least I didn't have to think about the vote. Reid had been on the outs for a long time. As far as I knew, he hadn't even been voting with the other guys. So, Reid was going home.

I hoped I could somehow get the next vote to go against Travis, so I could choose between two good options. Cameron vs Chris felt like a much different decision than Cam vs Travis.

I wasn't including Kyle.

He'd make it to the end, but our personalities absolutely didn't work together.

Anyway, Chris left me with his entire care package too. It was full to the brim with prepackaged desserts and candy. He apologized for not being able to pack real food, but that had been against the rules, apparently.

WHEN WE MADE it back to the island, I passed out desserts, melted chocolate, and lollipops for everyone to share. We all chatted and had a good time pigging out on sugar.

Afterward, we all felt like shit, and everyone crashed in the shelter. It was quite possibly the best day I'd ever had on the island.

EVERYONE WAS quiet again while we walked to the voting area. I was at the back of the line, and Kyle was the only guy stupid enough—or smart enough—to walk beside me.

It was the first time I'd been to the vote since that first day, but it was worse than the first one.

My heart sank as Rhett read the votes.

Chris

Reid

Chris

Chris

Chris

Reid was supposed to go home. How had the vote switched to Chris?

The only thing I could think of was the way I'd caught Cameron watching me laugh with Chris.

But Cam wouldn't have come up with the idea to vote out my only other good option, would he? If he was booted at four, after getting rid of Chris, I'd have to choose between Travis, Kyle, and Reid.

And *Travis* would've been the best option.

Travis.

So it couldn't have been Cam's idea.

...Right?

eleven

MOLLY

I DIDN'T SAY a word on the walk back to the shelter.

Or as I cuddled up in the blanket Travis had packed for me.

Travis, my possible future mate.

I was going to be sick.

I didn't want a mate at all. And now the one guy I somewhat trusted had probably broken my trust again.

So what the hell was I going to do?

Kyle walked over to my shelter and leaned up against the tree nearest to it. "What's going on, Doll?"

"For the love of all that is holy, stop calling me that," I said, staring up at the stars through the tree branches above us.

"I will if you will."

"I call you by your name," I said, flashing him a look.

"I mean that I'll call you Molly, if you tell me why I can't smell your pheromones anymore."

Squeezing my eyes shut, I let out a breath.

A long breath.

A long, long breath.

I wasn't ready to deal with Kyle right then.

"You were fucking Chris behind our backs, weren't you?" he asked.

"How would I possibly be having sex with anyone right now? You guys have at least two sets of eyes on me at all times, not including Rhett's," I shot back.

"Where there's a will, there's a way."

"That saying does *not* apply to this situation. I'm frustrated because you guys voted out one of my top candidates when I was under the impression that someone else was going home, okay? Now, just give me space."

"Alright." Kyle finally strode away, looking pretty proud of himself.

I wanted to throw something at the bastard.

A coconut, maybe.

Or something harder.

A rock would be good. A big, heavy rock.

I stayed where I was, still staring up at the sky.

Kyle went to sleep pretty fast.

For once, Travis and Reid did too.

None of them were suspicious of Cameron, which meant our plan had succeeded.

But the victory felt hollow.

After a little more time passed, Cam sat down near the base of my shelter, leaning up against a tree. "You're upset with me," he said.

"You were supposed to be on my team." My voice was quiet. "Tell me the Chris vote wasn't your idea."

"I can't lie to you, Lollipop."

My eyes stung. "He could've been my best chance at happiness."

"Your *second* best." There was an edge to Cam's voice. A hardness I hadn't heard before.

"You voted him out because you didn't want to compete with him." My sadness started to fade.

"Of course I did. I'm not here to watch you walk off with some other bastard."

"*Some other* implies that you're also a bastard."

"I never said I wasn't."

I sat up, anger in the lines of my face. "I *helped* you. I *trusted* you."

"And I'll take care of you for the rest of our lives in exchange."

I shook my head, shoving hair out of my eyes. "I don't want someone to *take care* of me. I don't want a guard, Cam. I want a partner."

"And I can't be that?"

"Do *not* start answering me with questions again. You were supposed to make it to the end so I could choose you."

He nodded. "I'm aware."

"It's not a choice if the other options are men you know I'd never consider tying myself to."

"Of course it is. It's just a controlled choice," Cam said, far too calmly.

I scoffed. "Whatever we had is over." I grabbed the care package he'd given me and dropped it on his lap before turning over in my shitty shelter.

My eyes stung, but he didn't say another word as I clutched my blanket to my chest and tried to will myself not to cry.

It didn't work.

THREE QUIET, tense days later, we finally made it to the last challenge. It was another puzzle—a massive 3D thing, with so many pieces I had to wonder exactly how big it was going to end up.

"Winner gets an automatic ride to the final three," Rhett said. "And spends tonight alone on a yacht with Molly."

I closed my eyes.

The last thing I wanted was to miss the final vote.

And removing one of four voters? It could screw with everything.

If Kyle won, it would be easy for Reid and Travis to get rid of Cam. If Reid won, there was every chance Kyle could decide to stick with Travis over Cameron too.

And after everything, I still hadn't decided who I was going to choose at the end. Choosing Cam was the safe but stupid choice. He'd made it clear that he was on his own side, not mine.

But the other men had too.

So where did that leave me?

In a shitstorm, *that* was where.

I pulled my long, tangled hair out of my eyes as the men got into position in front of the puzzles.

I had no idea which of them was going to win. Reid and Travis had done okay with the brainy challenges, though neither of them had actually won anything. Cam was almost always dead center, which told me he was aiming for that position.

There was a chance he was good at puzzles.

There was also a chance he wasn't.

Kyle didn't have a shot in hell, though. He was terrible at those kinds of things.

The challenge began at Rhett's command, and the men got to work.

As expected, Kyle didn't have a clue where to start and was aimlessly trying pieces, one after another.

Reid started sorting everything, which seemed like a decent route to take. No one knew what the puzzle was going to look like, so sorting might give him a clue or advantage of some kind.

Travis went ahead and started trying to fit pieces on the base of it like Kyle. His forehead was creased, and his lips pressed together in frustration as he tried piece after piece.

When I finally looked at Cam, my attention stopped there. And stayed.

He was moving through the puzzle quickly. There was no trial and error—he simply went through the pieces until he found the right one, and lined it up with the others easily.

He was already a third of the way through the puzzle, and no one else had a single piece.

I bit my lip as I watched him.

There was no reason for Cam to hold back anymore. If he won, he didn't have to participate in the vote. He was in the final three—which meant I could pick between him and two others.

Considering he'd gotten rid of Chris, the only other guy I somewhat liked, I didn't think he cared who he went up against.

The other guys started using Cam's puzzle as a guide, and finally managed to get a few pieces, but he was two-thirds of the way through it already. There wasn't a chance they would catch up.

And as he neared the end of it, I realized why it was so easy for him.

And my throat swelled.

He put in the last piece, the small freckle beside my left eye, and stepped back to study the statue of me.

The other guys stopped trying to solve their own puzzles.

Travis and Kyle were grimacing.

Reid was staring at Cameron with something akin to under-standing.

Cam was only looking at me.

I forced my gaze to land on Rhett.

He announced Cameron the winner, then guided us to a waiting speedboat. With one last look at the three guys headed for the final vote, I lifted a hand in a wave.

Then, I stepped onto the boat behind Cameron.

We'd done it.

We'd gotten him to the end.

But I still felt betrayed.

THE BENCH WAS SMALL, so our sides pressed together as the boat carried us to the yacht.

Cam had a backpack on his shoulders, and I knew it was the one I'd dropped on him the night before.

He might want to talk about that.

I wanted...

Well, I didn't know what I wanted.

Everything was screwed up.

We reached the yacht and were immediately guided to the dining room. They brought menus out, and we ordered. Cam was a lot hungrier than me, considering he hadn't gone on any of the food dates I'd been forced to attend.

It didn't surprise me at all when he ordered four different meals.

I went with two myself. Though I'd only manage one of the large servings, I'd seen enough starving supernatural men eat while on the island to know that he'd still be hungry after he was done with everything he'd ordered. Three probably would've been safer, but I didn't want to waste food when he could order more if he needed to.

"Can we please act like this is a normal meal back at the apartment for now, and have the conversation we know is coming after we eat?" Cam asked, setting his forearms on the large table. The yacht was moving, but I wasn't watching the scenery.

"A normal apartment meal for us would require you driving me insane," I said.

"*Flirtatiously* insane."

I rolled my eyes. "I'm not in the mood."

"Let's talk now, then."

"I'll never be in the mood for that," I grumbled.

Cam leaned over the table. "I didn't spend four years falling in love with you to risk watching you walk away with another man when there was something I could do about it. I'm not a gambler, Lolli. I knew I had Kyle and Travis in my pocket. I had them certain that I wasn't a real contender, and Reid was. I was making it to the end, and I wasn't taking the only other man you even somewhat liked with me."

"That's insanely selfish, Cam," I shot back.

I wasn't going anywhere near his comment about falling in love with me.

Not even maybe.

"Selfish, but smart," he said.

The servers arrived with our food, but Cam made no move to touch his.

I'd seen the single-minded focus most grown-ass fae men

had on the meals placed before them on the island. Him not digging in immediately was significant.

"You're frustrated because you feel like I haven't told you enough about myself," Cam said. "And you're right. I haven't. There are a lot of things I wasn't allowed to discuss, but there aren't any rules now. Ask me anything."

"Why haven't you touched your food?" I gestured to the many plates in front of him.

"You're hurt," he said. "That far outweighs a little hunger."

"A *little* hunger? You've been surviving on nothing but fish for nearly a month, Cam."

"I've been fighting every instinct that pushes me to protect you and claim you for nearly a month, too. That's been a hell of a lot harder than going hungry."

I sighed. "Fine, let's act like everything's normal and just eat. We can talk when I can't hear your stomach rumbling anymore."

He nodded, but didn't pick up his fork until I did.

There was a piece of chocolate cake on one of my plates, so I didn't hesitate before cutting into it. When the flavor hit my tongue, I groaned.

Loudly.

Cameron already had a forkful of grilled chicken in his mouth.

"Holy shit," I mumbled around the cake. It came out sounding more like "Oy it," but I was sure he'd get the message.

Still chewing, he leaned over and cut a piece of my cake for himself.

My lower belly tensed slightly at the intimacy, and my face warmed.

Cam inhaled deeply after swallowing. His fork was still full of cake. "That's what finally gets you wanting me again, Loll? Stealing your food?"

"Oh, shut up." I leaned across the table and took a big chunk of what looked like cheesecake from one of his plates, taking a bite of that. "Mine's better," I said.

He shook his head and cut another piece of chicken. "Try this."

When he handed me his fork, there was a bit of challenge in his eyes.

And I wasn't about to back down.

So, I took the fork and bit down myself.

"Okay, that's good," I agreed.

We focused on the food, sharing bites back and forth as we ate. I was full long before Cam was, but he managed to get me to try some of everything, even after I felt like I might burst.

When he was finally as stuffed as I was, we were escorted to our room at the top of the boat.

Everything was elegant and modern, with huge glass windows that looked out over the ocean and the rest of the scenery around us. We were moving slowly, and the boat's rocking was barely noticeable.

What *wasn't* barely noticeable?

The single gigantic bed in the center of the room. It had to be big enough for a fae man. Wings, horns, and all.

Cam walked over to the windows and peered out at the ocean, whistling. "Can't say I get tired of this view."

I headed straight for the large bathroom I could see connected to the room. "I'm going to wash the sand off my skin."

"Need help with that?"

I turned to glare at Cam, but the grin he wore told me he was joking.

I flipped him the bird on my way into the bathroom anyway, and locked the door behind me.

twelve

MOLLY

THE SHOWER WAS GLORIOUS.

By the time I finally emerged, I felt like a whole new person. My skin and hair were clean for the first time in a month. I'd found a toothbrush in there, so my teeth were too.

I hadn't found a change of clothes, and wasn't about to put that damn green bikini back on, so I just held my towel around my body as I padded to the bed.

Cam was still leaning against the wall near the window, keeping his sand away from the bed, which I appreciated tremendously.

And felt a little guilty about making him wait so long.

"All yours," I said, tucking my legs beneath the blankets.

His eyes lingered on me.

It was a solid two minutes before he finally disappeared into the bathroom.

Five minutes after that, he came out wrapped in a towel too.

I forced myself to turn on my side and stare out the windows, instead of at Cam.

He was going to want to talk about deep, important shit.

And we had never done that before. We'd never had a real, genuine conversation without sarcasm or teasing, unless you counted the one when I gave back his care package.

I wasn't ready for that.

It sounded... intense.

The bed dipped a little behind me. I assumed he made himself comfortable on the mattress beside me.

"Molly," he said.

The fact that he used my real name, and the serious tone of his voice, told me that honest conversation was coming in hot.

So, I changed the subject.

"You didn't warn me about the pheromones."

There was a moment's pause before he answered. I'd caught him off guard. "I was distracted watching you get off. It didn't occur to me until we were back at camp, and all the other guys were watching you."

"You looked proud of that."

He snorted. "Of course I was proud. The woman I'd wanted for years wanted me so much that her scent declared it loudly. It drove me fucking insane knowing that all of the other men were wondering if that scent was for them."

I rolled my eyes.

"You didn't let any of the others touch you, right?"

"What if I did?" I tossed back.

His chest rumbled with a quiet growl. "I'll fucking kill them."

"Guess I know why you were never on *Bachelorette*."

"It would've been my nightmare. Who touched you?"

"It's really not your business, Cam."

"Like hell it isn't." His hand landed on my hip, over the blanket, and he rolled me to my back. He was propped up on his side, tilted toward me, and his hot gaze met mine. "Who? It was Chris, wasn't it?"

I scowled. "I'm allowed to have secrets just as much as you are."

"All of my secrets are yours now," he growled back.

"Yeah, right."

"I told you, I'll answer all of your questions."

"I don't even know what questions to ask, Cam. You didn't tell me anything about fae, no one's explained the way a mate bond is formed, and I have no idea who you are outside of my sarcastic guard."

"Yet your scent is still singing for me."

"Fuck off."

His eyes flashed. "Roll over."

"Why would I—oof."

He rolled me onto my stomach and tugged the pillow out from under my face, so my cheek hit the mattress. "What the hell?" I grumbled into the sheets.

"You're tense," he said. "I can fix that."

"I didn't give you permission to—ohh." My groan was loud.

His hands had landed on my shoulders, his thumbs finding the knots in my muscles with ease.

"Good?" he asked.

"Very. Don't stop," I mumbled.

He made a noise of agreement, and continued rubbing my shoulders. "My parents lead the Society. They were elected nearly a millennium ago, and continue to be reelected every time another vote comes around."

My forehead creased, but smoothed when his thumbs dug into my muscles right where I needed them.

Another groan escaped me.

"I know you hate the Society. I can agree that the way they're doing things with compatible mates right now is screwed up, as well, but all of the Society's leaders have been in place for a very long time. They're not sure how to deal with all of the recent changes. They want to get out of their roles, but there aren't any other fae who are known and liked as widely as they are. They're trapped," Cameron said.

The idea of ancient fae leaders being trapped was ridiculous to me, but I was too busy enjoying the massage to say as much.

"I've been urged for centuries to find a mate and take their place, by them, and many other powerful fae. I told you I had connections. That's why. I'm liked and respected across the Society, but mortal fae can't rule."

"Holy shit," I swore. My voice was still muffled by the bed.

Cam was going to be their next *king*. Or Society leader, I supposed, but it sounded similar to me.

"How did you end up guarding me, then? Aren't you close to dying?"

He made a noise of agreement. "I've been fading for a while. If you and I don't seal a bond, I'll only make it a few more weeks."

My stomach tensed.

He worked my knots harder.

"My parents sat me down four years ago and told me in no uncertain terms that they were tired of waiting for me to choose a mate myself. They would use their power in the

Society to force me into every game show there was until I secured a match. They knew very well that I was never going to mate with a female I didn't know and care for before a game, so when I offered an alternative, they accepted. I proposed choosing a compatible female to guard until her game show arose, and winning her heart on the *Bachelorette*."

"This is no fucking *Bachelorette*," I said.

He chuckled. "Their left-hand fae realized my plan a few weeks ago, and claimed it was stacking the odds in my favor too obviously. There would be bloodshed. This was their answer. Being your guard and having the connections I do turned me from a shoo-in on *Bachelorette* to *Survival's* biggest target. When I win, everyone will know damn well that I did because I outsmarted them. With the help of my mate, of course."

I scowled into the bed, but the scowl faded as he continued working my muscles. "Why didn't your parents just assign you a mate or something if they were that concerned?"

"Fae don't work that way. Mental magic abounds—everyone would know the truth, and all three of us would've been killed. There are rules to follow, and the rulers must follow them more exactly than everyone else."

"So what happens if we *do* seal the bond?"

"Whatever we want to happen."

"Cameron," I argued, knowing that wasn't the full truth.

He chuckled. "I'm serious, Lolli. We can do whatever we want."

"But?"

"But there is some expectation that we would go to my parents' side and work with them until the next election, when we would most-likely take over running the Society."

"That's insane."

"I'm aware. It's just an option, though."

"Could you turn it down if they elected you even though you didn't want it?"

"Not quite. *We* would be magically bound to the role if the majority voted us into it. That aspect of fae democracy was sealed with magic from the beginning of time."

"So if we seal the bond, we're going to end up ruling the Society."

"It's not certain, but it is likely," he admitted.

I squeezed my eyes shut. "You should've told me that before I started working with you. You know how I feel about the Society, Cam."

"I know how you feel about how the Society has treated you," he agreed. "And if we were to rule, we could change everything about the way the compatible mates are treated before the game shows."

"Could we get rid of the game shows altogether?" I asked.

"It's unlikely. There aren't enough compatible mates to keep all of us alive, so this is the fair way to do it," he admitted. "It also helps human perception of us, which is important. It would be easy for them to start seeing us as monsters. The shows humanize us to them."

He wasn't wrong about that.

All of the humans I knew *adored* fae. Some of them would even bring Cam coffee or croissants at my last job, without bringing anything for me.

They had saved our world, and given us something fun to focus on through the *Bachelorette*. That alone was enough to win most of us over.

"They're not going to keep going with Survival though, are they?" I asked. "Bachelorette is much fairer for the women involved."

"I'm not sure. If it's highly regarded, I would imagine they're going to keep it going."

"Could we change that if we mated?"

I didn't want any other women to get trapped on the island like I had. Not when the alternative was getting to choose their own mate on the other show.

"I don't know. The Society's rulers are not all-powerful. They work with two other couples, their right and left hands, to keep each other in check. If we could convince the right and left hands to change it, then yes. Undoubtedly. But we would still have the problem of dying male fae who are unwilling to play *Bachelorette*."

"Like you."

"Like me," he agreed.

"Are any of the other guys as close to dying as you are?"

"No. Rhett's the closest, but he has no desire to take a mate. He's a few months younger than me, and plans to let himself fade."

I sighed. "I like him, even though he threw me out of a plane."

Cam chuckled. "You like me more."

"Do I?" I drawled, using his go-to avoidance technique.

"You do." He dug his thumbs into my shoulders again, and I bit back another groan.

"You're too good at this. How many other women have you massaged?"

He snorted. "None. I watched instruction videos a few times. Promised myself I'd be able to use them one day. It about killed me not to be able to hold you or touch you every time they looked you over for a promotion because of me."

"Not because of *you*."

"You were always mine, so yeah, because of me."

"You're giving yourself too much credit."

He chuckled. "And I don't usually?"

My lips curved upward. "How did you realize the puzzle was a statue of me?"

"I've spent four years staring at you, Lollipop. I've memorized as much of you as you've let me."

My face warmed at the words.

He was slyly mentioning that he'd never seen me naked.

"If you hadn't been assigned to protect me, I'd have to call you my stalker," I said into the sheets.

He laughed. "I'd wear the title with honor."

"I'm sure you would." A moment passed, and my amusement faded as I remembered him voting Chris off just because I didn't hate the guy.

While I did understand his perspective of being unwilling to risk losing, it had been dangerous to remove the only guy other than him that I sort of jived with.

"Your pheromones are fading while I'm touching you, Lolli. Where's your head?"

"My head? Right here."

"You know I mean your thoughts."

I sighed. "It feels like an attack to vote out Chris just because he made me laugh once. It's not like we were close. He just made a decent argument."

"My jealousy aside," Cam said, and my eyebrows lifted. "I don't trust Chris."

Jealousy?

He was admitting to jealousy?

He added, "As much as you dislike Kyle, Reid, and Travis, and as difficult as they are, I'd much sooner put my life and yours in their hands. I would trust them to keep you safe."

"Kyle doesn't even plan on letting his mate work," I argued.

"Kyle wants to stay alive, and knows as well as any fae male that if his mate says run, he'll ask her how far."

"So I should choose him?" I drawled.

Cam laughed humorlessly. "If you want me to kill him."

I rolled my eyes. "I've never seen you violent before. Every other guy on this island is more aggressive than you."

"Every other guy on this island has the freedom to play the game however he wants. For me, there was only one path to victory. I played the role I had to play to get here, first as your guard, and then as a man you despised."

"Are you telling me that I don't know you? Because that doesn't exactly make me want to choose you, Cam."

His thumbs grew rougher against my back, and the feeling was incredible. "In a choice between me, Travis, and Kyle, we both know I'm your only logical option."

He was right.

It pissed me off that he was, but that didn't change the truth.

"So?" I finally asked.

"So, we're going to be mates. There's no point in hoping for another outcome anymore."

I'd never hoped for another outcome.

I just hadn't wrapped my mind around the one I now had to deal with.

Cameron Cassette was going to be my mate, for better or worse.

And I knew even less about him than I'd thought.

thirteen

MOLLY

WHEN MY SHOULDERS had officially turned to mush under Cam's skilled hands, I rolled to my back again and grabbed the TV remote off the nightstand beside the bed. There was a television on the wall, and watching a movie seemed safer than talking to Cameron anymore.

He didn't exactly have anything comforting to say.

I turned a movie on, and he didn't protest against it as I did.

When I scooted back to lean against the bed's wooden headboard, however, I discovered my conundrum.

There were only two pillows, and Cam had already tucked both of them behind his back.

"You're an asshole," I said, slumping against the rough, hard wood as the movie started.

"A *clever* asshole."

I flipped him off.

"Don't tempt me, Lolli."

He relaxed against both of his gigantic pillows while I tried to ignore my discomfort.

A few minutes into the movie, my lower back was too tight to remain where I was. I finally plopped down on the mattress on my stomach, propping my face up with my hands.

Cam tugged my towel down the back of my thighs, and my foot kicked out of its own volition, ready to defend me.

He caught my ankle quickly. "Easy, Loll. I didn't think you wanted me staring up your towel while you watched the movie, so I pulled it down. That's all."

My face flushed.

Wetness gathered between my thighs.

"Thanks," I finally said, not looking back at him.

Making eye contact would only make me hornier. Or more embarrassed.

Or both.

"Mmhm." He dragged his thumb over the outside of my ankle slowly before he released it.

I pressed my knees together as I lowered my feet to the mattress.

Cam's hand landed lightly on the back of my thigh, and though my hips arched slightly, I didn't tell him to move it.

His touch was warm, and his hand felt ridiculously good. It was far enough down that I didn't think he was going to try to feel me up or anything.

"For the record," he said, as I finally tried to focus on the movie. "I'm more than willing to share my pillow setup. No asking required."

I rolled my eyes.

I MADE it another twenty minutes before my neck hurt too much to stay where I was.

It was time to accept defeat.

Cam had outsmarted me.

And I was still wet between my thighs, despite the old superhero movie playing on the screen. It didn't help that every time they showed a sexy man, I was reminded of how much hotter Cameron was.

Reminded of how I'd been plastered to his shirtless body, riding his cock through our clothes, too.

With a sigh, I finally lifted myself off the mattress and positioned my side against his. He was in the middle of the pillows, and as expected, didn't scoot over to make extra space for me.

He did roll onto his side, though, making it easy for me to press my hip against his abs as I tried to get comfortable.

His fingers slipped into my hair as I watched the movie. They felt so damn good on my scalp, massaging lightly, that I didn't tell him to stop.

After a few minutes, his nose brushed my cheek as he dipped his head toward my ear and murmured, "Your towel rode up again. Want me to fix it for you?"

My head jerked upward, and I saw the edge of it pulled up to my bare hip. My core was still covered, just barely, but one of my arms was trapped beneath a pillow. The other was folded up over my chest, holding the towel over my breasts so it wouldn't get pinned between me and Cam.

"Fine," I said.

My eyes followed his fingers down my front, and my core squeezed tightly at the sight of his hand so close to where I wanted it.

I tried to refocus on the movie as he let go of the towel, but my mind remained on him.

And what we'd done on the beach.

And what I knew about mating.

"Kyle said a mate bond is formed with magic and sex," I said, when I couldn't stay quiet any longer. The movie was still playing, but that superhero didn't hold a candle to the gorgeous fae beside me.

Literally, when you factored in Cam's fire.

"If you want answers about that, you're going to have to tell me which of the men you let touch you." He lowered his lips to my ear and caught my lobe between his teeth, tugging lightly at the single piercing there.

My body clenched again. "That's not fair."

"It's *absolutely* fair. I deserve to know how many males I need to erase from your memory with my hands, mouth, and cock."

I squeezed my thighs together tighter.

The soft growl that followed told me Cam could smell how much his words had turned me on.

His fingers tightened in my hair, his other hand landing on my thigh again.

This time, it slid upward just enough to make me squeeze my legs together more tightly.

"You're drenched for me, Lollipop. I can smell it. Tell me what I want to know, and I'll do the same for you."

I let out an unsteady breath.

"That's not a good enough deal," I said. "What else will you give me?"

"What do you want?"

The words brought me back to the beach, and the time he bargained for a hug.

"My own pillow," I lied.

He chuckled. "Are you sure?" His hand slid higher, the side of his palm nearly brushing my aching core.

"Positive."

His teeth tugged my ear lightly. "Alright. You first."

I sucked in a breath as he moved his hand again. My clit was nearly *throbbing* with need. It was driving me insane.

"None of them touched me," I finally said, closing my eyes in an attempt to regain control of my body. "I didn't let any of them."

He rumbled.

The sound was hot, carnal satisfaction. "Good girl."

My hips arched.

Having him so close to touching me, but so far, was *torture*.

"A mate bond begins with penetrative sex," he said, his lips brushing my earlobe again as he spoke. His thumb dragged slowly over the front of my thigh, making my hips jerk. "My cock will enter you, when you're good and wet for me. I'll be much bigger than the human males you were with years ago. It will take time to adjust. When I've filled you entirely, we will exchange vows. The words are simple, but powerful. *'I am yours'*. Our shared release following the vows will give you a portion of my magic. The bond will be permanent after that, but the actual change from human to fae is a process that will take a few weeks. Three to four, usually. Sometimes longer. Sometimes shorter."

"What's the process?" I asked, tensing as I waited for him tell me that it required pain, or blood, or some kind of sacrifice.

His lips curved upward.

His thumb dragged over the front of my thigh again, making me arch a little more.

"Your body won't be prepared to take your whole portion of my power at once. The first time we're together after the vows will ignite the change, but you'll need more magic to fuel it when you've burned through what I've given you. The need will feel similar to hunger as you become fae. Lust will set in when you need more of my magic, and we'll fuck until you have what you need."

I let out a long breath. "Wow. Can't say I was expecting that."

He chuckled.

"The other guys did proposition me, though. Having sex with them wouldn't have started a bond, would it?" I asked.

"No. The vows come first. You have to choose to take a mate before he can give you his power."

Give me his power... with his cock.

Fantastic.

I squeezed my thighs together, and the motion forced his hand just a little higher. The edge of his pinky was up against my clit. Though the touch was light, it made me want more.

"What's the point of the pheromones, then?" I asked, my voice wobbling a bit.

"Your body was created to be fae, it just lacks the magic needed to get there. The pheromones tell us that you're ready to change."

Right.

"So after the game is over, what happens? I choose... someone... and we go back to their house and have a lot of sex?"

"The Society purchased a large beach house on an island not far from here. It'll be ours for the week following the end of the game. The first week of the change is supposed to be the most intense. After that, it's manageable."

"How will I change, exactly?"

"My magic will be equally yours. You'll burn with fire, in here." He freed his hands from between my thighs, trailing it up the front of my towel until he tapped the center of my chest.

My legs clenched tighter.

"You'll develop wings, here." His hand slid beneath my shoulders, lightly tracing a line over my spine. "Shifting back to human form will take time. You'll slowly transition to your fae form as the change occurs, and there's no way to switch back until after it's through. Even then, it will be difficult. It's usually two to three months before you can see this version of yourself in the mirror again."

"What does it feel like to have wings?"

"Powerful."

A shiver rolled down my spine.

His lips curved upward. "Sensual, too. You'll like it, Lolli."

"How is it sensual?"

"Wings are erogenous zones. They make you stronger, but expose you as well."

"Can I feel yours?"

"Of course." He didn't bother sitting up. A moment later, his wings were spread out behind us, his horns curving off his head. "You know how my body will react."

I warmed with the reminder of the way I'd touched his wings on the beach. His cock had throbbed hard beneath me.

He could smell how much I wanted him, so it wouldn't kill him to deal with an erection.

Reaching out, I dragged my fingertips lightly over the silken feathers of his gorgeous, golden wings. He tensed beneath me, his grip on my hair tightening.

His free hand landed on my abdomen over the towel, and pressed down lightly as if he was trying to stop himself from touching me.

"Are the cameras watching?" I whispered.

"I'm sure they are," he gritted out. "There are no blinds to pull down over the windows. I checked.

"Maybe we should pull the blanket over us?"

He got it out from beneath us, covering our bodies with it from my breasts down even though we both still had towels on.

When he moved, his erection brushed my hip, hard and thick.

"You didn't walk around naked on the beach," I said, my hand still on his wing.

"Didn't want to make you drool, or put a target on my back just because I've got the biggest package."

I snorted, and he winked.

"Are they more sensitive at your back or closer to the tip?" I asked, moving my fingers to the place they connected to his back.

"Tip."

I started making my way over, and his body grew stiffer beneath mine.

His grip on my hair tightened even more. It was almost painful—but surprisingly enough, I liked the feeling.

"Easy," he gritted out, as I touched the feathers there.

"Why? Are you close to losing control?" I leaned against his erection lightly.

It was bigger than it had been a minute earlier.
Much bigger.

It had already popped free of the towel. If I moved mine, we'd be bare together.

"Closer than I should be when I can smell your unfulfilled need."

He wasn't wrong there.

I was soaked.

But I wanted to push him just a little further, so I rolled onto my side and draped half my body over his. Pressing my thigh over his massive cock, I reached for his horns.

He growled, low and warning. "If your breasts break free of that towel, I *will* have to fuck them with my mouth. Cameras be damned."

My body flushed.

My desire dripped down my thigh, wetting his erection, and he swore viciously.

I finally touched the tips of his horns, my towel falling open as I did.

A snarl erupted from his chest.

In a heartbeat, he had me rolled over and pinned to my back.

My towel was open wide, my bare body covered by both his and the blanket.

His erection was between my thighs, the thick length of it pressed against my center.

"You are *mine*, Lolli. Do you understand?"

The intensity of the words finally registered. He'd said them before—but I hadn't known about the mating process.

Now that I did?

I knew he was bringing up the bond.

The permanent mate bond.

"I'm yours," I whispered, and his eyes absolutely blazed.

It wasn't a vow.

He wasn't inside me, like he would have to be for that to happen.

But it was a reminder of what was to come. As much as I'd fought it, and as much as I'd been hurt, we both knew there was no alternative for me.

I was his.

And he was going to be mine.

Our gazes were locked.

He lowered his mouth to one of my breasts and said against me, "This is mine."

"Yours."

He slowly traced a circle around my nipple with the tip of his tongue.

Our eyes remained locked as he dragged his tongue over the next breast, before trailing down my abdomen. His horns held the blanket high enough to keep me exposed for him, but low enough that the cameras couldn't see our bodies through the windows.

When he finally brushed a kiss to my clit, his eyes still hot and heavy, he said again, "*Mine*."

"Yours," I breathed.

His tongue traced a slow circle around my clit, but I couldn't watch that.

I was too busy watching the lust in his eyes.

He licked and teased, dragging me to the edge of a climax and pausing while I panted and rocked, desperate for release. "When you come on my mouth," he said, his lips brushing my clit. "You'll come knowing that you belong to me for the rest of our immortal lives, Lollipop. Understand?"

"Yes." I was too close to unraveling to even consider saying anything else.

His lips curved upward slowly.

And he finally focused on my clit again.

I cried out, bucking and arching as he brought me the release I so desperately needed. The pleasure rolled all the way from my head and to my toes—and I wanted more.

Needed more.

Cameron sucked on the inside of my thigh as I came down from the climax, panting hard. "I'm not risking putting your pleasure on camera anymore. If you need to get off again before the end of the game, or the end of the night, you do so in my arms. While I conceal you from watching eyes."

"I don't *need* to come again," I said, still trying to catch my breath.

"You want to." He climbed out from beneath the blanket and tucked my bare body against his chest. His cock was rock hard, but he didn't ask me to take care of it. "Which is just as valid as a need in my book."

"I haven't gotten you off," I countered. "You want to, don't you?"

"Not as much as I want to feel you climax against me again."

I scowled. "Cam."

He chuckled. "I've waited four years for this, Lolli. I can wait four more days for the release I want."

"I thought wants were just as important as needs."

"Yours are." He nipped at my bottom lip. "Mine are better suited for waiting until after the cameras are gone."

"If you're not getting off, then I'm not either," I warned.

"Stubborn woman." He kissed me lightly.

"If we're not fucking tonight," I said, "Then you'd better give me more details about the Society. Where they're located. Where we'd be expected to live if we seal the bond."

"*After* we've sealed the bond." He didn't like hearing me talk like it was still just a possibility.

"After," I corrected myself.

There was no point in playing games anymore.

He'd won, and we both knew it.

"*After* we've sealed the bond." He didn't like hearing me talk like it was still just a possibility.

"After," I corrected myself.

fourteen

MOLLY

I SETTLED against Cameron's bare chest, and he slid his fingers back through my hair. "The Society isn't stationed in just one location. They own three homes in every place they rotate between, and there's no required order that they have to visit. They go where they feel they can be the most effective."

"*Three* homes?" I asked.

"The leading couple works as one with their right and left hands, remember?"

"The right and left hands are the other two couples?"

"Mmhm."

"Are they also elected?" I asked.

"They are. The current right hands have no children, and keep to themselves for the most part. The lefts are loosely related to Chris. They aren't much liked, but the last couple in their position was Rhett's family. They lost their lives in the human war, and the current pair were the runners-up in the last election."

"Shit," I murmured. "No wonder you and Rhett are close, if you grew up together while both of your parents led the Society."

Cameron nodded. "In an ideal world, Rhett and his mate would take his parents' place when we take mine. That would require him winning a mate, though, and he's grown even more volatile in his age than I have. On top of that, he has no desire to compete."

"He didn't seem volatile to me. You don't either."

"Not *dangerous*, volatile. *Possessive*, volatile. Fae grow more beastly as we age alone. It's the instinct to survive pushing us to find and claim a partner before it's too late. We have little control over it, but it affects some more than others."

"And Rhett is one of them?"

"Yes."

"And even if he wants to, he can't go on Bachelorette if he's that possessive," I said.

"Nope."

"Were his parents as involved as yours? If they were still here, would they make him take a mate somehow?"

"They were worse than mine." He flashed me a small grin. "My parents have decided he's their second son since his parents passed. I'd put a lot of money on them somehow forcing him to play Survival in the next season or two."

Which meant at least one more woman was going to be trapped in my position.

"Would they let us warn the woman, at least? I don't want anyone else being suddenly forced into this if there's something we can do about it."

"Not before the next season. We'll need to seal the bond as soon as we leave the island, and we won't be functioning in Society that first week or two afterward. They won't wait more than a few days before starting the next game."

"We could seal the bond after we talk to your parents," I suggested.

Cam chuckled. "No can do, Lolli. I'm making you mine the moment I've won."

My face warmed. "Rhett told me they started playing our season on TV already. So the next girl will probably have an idea it's a possibility, at least. She might even have time to strategize."

A moment passed, my thoughts still turning. "If Rhett won, would he get elected like you?"

"Like *us*, yes. Quickly," he agreed. "Rhett is very well-liked, but all of fae Society knows he's determined not to take a mate, which makes getting elected impossible."

My forehead creased. "Why is he so against it? I thought he needs a mate to survive."

"He fell in love with a human a long time ago. Decided he wanted to marry her. He proposed, and she said yes. When he told her what he was a few weeks later, and that he wouldn't age when she did, she was horrified. Threw the ring at him and ended it immediately. She died a few years back, and he went to the funeral, still in love with her. He'd rather fade than tie himself to anyone else."

"Holy shit."

"Fae love deeply, and intensely. It's how we're made."

"Guess it's a good thing for you that you made sure I'm yours," I said.

He chuckled. "A damn good thing."

"How are we playing it when we get back to the beach?" I asked.

"We're done playing. We already won the game. When we go back, everyone will realize you're mine. I'll tell them I managed to seduce you while we were on the boat."

"If we keep it a secret, it could help the girl in the next season," I countered. "What if her guard is brought in too?"

"If that happens, he'll be the first to go no matter what he says or does. No one would let this happen again."

My lips curved upward. "I guess not."

"We may have ruined someone else's plans, though. Good work." He kissed my forehead, and I laughed.

"You're an ass."

"A *clever* ass."

I couldn't deny that.

WE SPENT the rest of the evening watching a movie while snuggled up together, then fell asleep in each other's arms.

EARLY THE NEXT MORNING, Rhett knocked on the door and said it was time to go back to the island.

Though I knew it was a little ridiculous, Cameron and I hadn't been walking around naked together. So, I wrapped myself in a towel before I went back to the bathroom for the despised green bikini. I tossed Cam's shorts out too, and his chuckle told me he got the message.

He was dressed and waiting when I emerged. Leaning up against the wall in nothing but those shorts, he was chest-achingly gorgeous. My yellow sweatshirt was hanging over his arm, waiting for me.

His lips curved when he saw me. "Good to see you in your favorite outfit again."

I swatted him on the arm with the back of my hand. "I'm burning it as soon as we're off the island. And never wearing a bra again."

"I approve of this plan."

"Shocking."

He chuckled, and handed me the sweatshirt. "Now that we don't have to hide anything, you can wear this."

"I can finally cover my tits? It's a miracle." I pulled it over my head and wrapped my arms around myself. "This is true bliss. Screw bikinis and tiny shorts."

Cam grinned and captured my hand, leading me toward the door. Rhett had his hand lifted, ready to knock again, when we emerged.

He tucked his hands in his pockets. "Ready?"

"Ready for it to be over," I said, pulling my hair off my face with my free hand. I should've braided it or tied it up. My hair tie was around my wrist, but I hadn't taken the time to use it.

We followed Rhett out to the speedboat connected to the yacht, and sat together on the tiny bench again. Cameron's arm was around my waist as we went, but my hair kept smacking him in the face.

"Sorry," I called out, after a particularly violent bump. "Forgot to put it up."

He laughed and snagged the band from my wrist. When he gathered all my hair for a high ponytail and smoothed the wild strands down, I bit my lip.

The man tied it without a problem, then put his arm around me again

It was sweet.

Really sweet.

The boat docked soon enough, and it didn't take long to confirm that Cam was right about Reid going home.

Cam and Kyle had been controlling the game—but considering Kyle hadn't had a clue about my relationship with Cam, Cam had outsmarted everyone.

As guilty as I felt for playing them, that was what the game was about. And since no one on the island had been outraged that *I* was the game show's grand prize, the guilt was shallow.

"Ready?" Cameron murmured into my ear, as he held my hand to help me out of the boat.

He didn't need to worry about showing affection anymore.

The game had changed.

They weren't competing against each other. They were competing *for* me.

Unfortunately for them, I'd already decided who the winner was going to be.

Cam didn't release my hand as we walked up onto the beach. I was a little warm in my sunshine sweatshirt, but it was that much less skin to apply sunblock to. So, I'd take the heat.

Travis looked confused, his forehead creasing at our intertwined fingers.

Kyle's eyes narrowed.

"Hey," Cam greeted them.

"What did you do?" Kyle growled.

"Oh, just enjoyed my Lollipop." Cameron's grin was wicked.

My face flushed at what he'd implied, but he wasn't wrong.

Two sets of nostrils flared as the men sniffed me, looking for evidence.

Their eyes darkened when they found it.

Cam's grin widened.

The bastards could obviously smell him on me. I should've showered before going back into the game.

Then again, Cam had wanted to claim me that way. If I'd tried to wash his scent off my skin, he probably would've done whatever he needed to reapply it.

Reapply it.

Like it was sunblock.

Which I was also absolutely and completely tired of.

Reapply obviously wasn't the right term, but whatever.

Anyway, I really wanted to smack him for that nickname right about then. Even though I'd grown to like it for the most part.

Neither of the men said another word as Cam led me to the fire. Or as we took a seat in front of it.

I leaned against his side and he toyed with my hair, neither of us saying much. Talking while the others listened wasn't quite what we wanted.

After a while, Kyle walked up.

Still naked.

He cleared his throat. "Dolly," he began.

The look I leveled him with made him sigh. "Molly. Can I talk to you for a minute?"

We'd had plenty of *minutes* to talk on the many dates he'd won, and I really wasn't interested in spending any more with him. But I didn't want to be a bitch, so I nodded anyway.

Cameron's grip on my hand tightened slightly, and I squeezed to reassure him before pulling free.

I wrapped my sweater-covered arms around my middle so Kyle wouldn't try to grab my hand like Cam had. Kyle had never done anything entirely inappropriate, but he was definitely a touchy guy.

We walked down the beach in silence, but I didn't go far enough that Cameron couldn't see me. I didn't want him worrying. The possessiveness he'd brought up as part of fae getting older made me want to go easy on the guy.

Even though I still didn't feel like I knew him well enough to become his mate.

"So, you and Cassette," Kyle said.

As much as I was used to not looking at him when he spoke, I really wished the guy would start wearing pants again.

"Yep."

He whistled. "I was under the impression that you hated him for lying to you."

"I did," I said.

It wasn't untrue.

I had hated him... for a few minutes.

I'd just been forced to move on because I had bigger problems than him not telling me exactly what was going to happen when I left the apartment with Rhett.

Survival was the bigger problem.

Kyle was a part of that.

"How did that change?"

"He apologized." I continued walking slowly beside Kyle, glancing over my shoulder to make sure Cam could still see me. He was relaxed by the fire, in the same place I'd left him. Despite his body position, I knew he was tense on the inside.

"That's it?"

"I'm a pretty simple woman," I said. "A genuine apology does wonders. When I gave Cameron a chance to explain himself, he told me the truth about not being allowed to share anything he knew. He had his mind combed before he came, to make sure nothing about guarding me gave him an advantage. If anything, it gave him a disadvantage because all of you knew he knew me. Some of the guys targeted him at the beginning, remember?"

Kyle nodded, though his expression was tight.

Frustrated, too.

"So, if I apologized..." He trailed off, waiting for me to finish the sentence.

"You'd have to know what to apologize for." My lips curved upward just slightly.

He grimaced.

"I think you know as well as I do that we wouldn't be happy together, Kyle. You're a pain in my ass, but you're not a bad guy. You deserve to find a woman you'd actually fit with. Maybe someone... cheerier than me?"

"I helped Cam get here. At least the bastard will owe me after this."

I gave him a knowing look. "You helped him get here because you didn't think there was a chance I'd ever consider choosing him."

"Maybe," Kyle grumbled.

I smiled. "*Definitely*. Have you ever thought about going on *Bachelorette*? I think you'd do pretty well there."

"Would if I could. The possessiveness is too dangerous." He shook his head. "I'll just have to come back here and win the next girl."

"Well, don't give up," I said.

He raised his eyebrows at me. "You do know who you're talking to, right?"

I laughed. "I know. It just seemed like the right thing to say."

"Cassette looks like he's ready to strangle me. What do you say you kiss me, just to get back at him for using me?" Kyle said, flashing me a devilish grin.

A snort escaped me. "In your dreams, buddy."

With that, I strode back to Cameron.

Kyle called after me, "If you meet the next girl, put in a good word for me!"

I flipped him off over my shoulder, and he laughed loudly.

Eventually, he'd be a great mate for someone who liked a loud, confident guy.

But he'd have to prove that to her himself. I sure as hell wasn't getting involved.

There was a crease between Cameron's brows when I walked back to him. "What did he say?" Cam asked, draping his arm over my shoulder and pulling me back to his side.

"We're in love, and I'm going to carry his children."

Cam growled, his grip on me tightening. "*Lolli*."

My lips curved upward. "He knows you outsmarted him. He asked me to put in a word with the next girl, if I meet her."

"And?"

"And I'm sure you saw me flip him off. If he wants a mate, he'll have to win her over himself."

Cam nodded.

His mood was more reserved than it had been when we were on the yacht and the speedboat, though.

Something told me he was nervous.

It was ridiculous for him to worry after I'd already agreed to be his, but I *did* get it. There was still no guarantee. And Travis and Kyle still *did* want me to choose them. If I was in love with a guy who could reject me that easily, I'd be stressed too.

"You don't think Travis would try to use his magic on me, right?" I asked.

Cam snorted. "He saw how fast Oren died. I don't think anyone will ever be stupid enough to try that on this island again. Travis isn't bright, but he doesn't have a death wish. He'll want to keep coming back here until he's won a mate or faded too much to try."

I settled against him.

It was going to be a long few days, especially if Cam remained stressed and quiet for parts of it... but we were going to make it.

Cam nodded.

His mood was more reserved than it had been when we were on the yacht and in the speedboat, though.

Something told me he was nervous.

It was difficult for him to worry after I'd already spread my bet his, but I did get it. There was still no guarantee that Travis and Kyle still did want me to choose them. If I was in love with a guy who could reject me that easily, I'd be a sad boy.

"You don't think Travis would try to use his music on me right?" I asked.

Cam snorted. "He saw how fast Oren died. I don't think anyone will ever be scared enough to try anon this island again, at least not for that. But the deep powers each have a way. He'll want to keep coming back here until there's were ended too much to buy."

I pulled against him.

It was going to be a long, long row. Luckily it remained stressed and quicker parts of me, but we were going to make it.

I STARED up at the stars through the trees above our head. Molly was curled up in my arms, her perfect body pressed against mine beneath her blanket. She'd had a conversation with Travis as well, and he'd accepted the truth with as much grace as Kyle had.

Both of the bastards were pissed with me, but they'd known there was a good chance they wouldn't win before they ever stepped foot on the island.

All of us did.

When night arrived, Kyle had sprawled out in the group's shelter.

Travis had claimed mine.

I would've rather taken Molly to my own, but I wasn't about to let another asshole sleep in my female's bed. Smelling her scent on his skin would drive me mad. So, we'd gone to bed in hers.

That had been hours earlier, though.

I hadn't managed to fall asleep. Not that I'd gotten much sleep on the island at all. Knowing I was moments away from losing Molly at all times kept my mind too occupied to rest until my body decided to shut down.

I was going to win the game—but it wasn't over yet.

And I wouldn't be able to relax until she was mine.

Permanently.

Molly shifted beside me, and my wings curved with her.

She didn't have my magic yet, but my body already responded to hers. It had from the beginning. Guarding her had been a simple task, because I'd felt like she was a part of me since the moment we met. I was aware of her every move, every sound, and every breath.

She lifted her head, eyes heavy with sleep. I'd only seen her like that twice during our four years. Both times were when she'd fallen asleep on the couch, watching a movie or TV show.

"Still awake?" she murmured.

My cock throbbed hard against her thigh. I couldn't have stopped it if I tried. I hadn't softened since I had her bare body against mine on that yacht.

"Yep." I kissed her forehead.

The alternative was to drag her up my body and make love to her mouth with mine. Which I didn't think she wanted, given she'd been sleeping moments earlier. And the hesitation I'd seen on her face so many times was definitely a deterrent.

Though I believed she was going to choose me, given the lack of other options, I knew she was still hesitant about it. And that was where my uncertainty came in.

"You're tense. Why?" Her voice was soft enough not to wake up Kyle or Travis. They were both snoring loudly enough that I had no doubts about it.

"Just tired of this island." I smoothed my hand over her back. The sweater she still had on prevented me from touching that soft, sexy skin. "Don't worry about it. Go back to sleep."

She rolled her eyes at me. "I thought you wanted me to be your mate."

"Of course I do." My voice came out as more of a growl than I intended.

"Then you have to tell me the full truth. I'm not doing a one-sided relationship."

I grimaced.

I'd known that was coming, just hoped I had a little more time first. I didn't want her worrying about me, or the state of our connection.

"Knowing that you could still choose one of the other males makes it difficult to relax," I admitted.

She nodded. "You don't trust me."

"It's not a lack of trust, per se, but—"

"It is, though. Trust takes time. And I've been avoiding you as much as you've been avoiding me for the past few weeks. We had to do it, but it doesn't make either of us confident in what we have." Her voice was still soft, those brown eyes warm as they looked into mine.

I nodded grudgingly.

She moved her thigh over my cock just a little, and I grunted.

"How much sleep have you gotten since we've been here?" she asked.

"Some."

"Cam," she warned.

"Not much," I finally admitted.

Molly nodded. "I think I can help with that."

My forehead creased.

She rolled to the side a bit, removing her body from mine. Though I wanted to pull her back against me and trap her there, I knew I couldn't. She needed her freedom.

My body clenched tighter with the realization that she was going to walk away.

Would she join Kyle in the shelter?

Or go to Travis's side, and—

A quiet hiss escaped me when a small, warm hand wrapped around my erection over the top of my shorts.

That, I hadn't expected.

Or even considered a possibility.

She rolled closer, so the front of her body was pressed against my side. "Is this okay?" she whispered, stroking me lightly through my shorts.

"Fuck, yes."

Her lips curved upward, and she pressed a kiss to the side of my throat.

My cock jerked in her hand, and I felt her smile widen.

She released me, slipping her fingers beneath my shorts. "I'm not very good at this, so tell me if I do something wrong."

"Not possible, Lolli." I slid one of my hands into her hair, screwing up the ponytail I'd tied for her earlier.

I'd fix it again after.

She wrapped her fingers around my bare cock. Thankfully, I managed to muffle my groan with her hair.

"How's that?" she asked.

"Perfect." The word was growled into her hair.

Her hips rocked against me slightly. I wanted to put a thigh between her legs to give her something to rub up against, but I wasn't doing a damn thing to risk stopping her when she touched me like that.

After she was done, I'd make sure she got more than she gave.

"You're massive," she whispered against me, slowly stroking my length. Her touch was soft and smooth, and it had been far too long since I received or gave myself any kind of pleasure. I wouldn't last long. "How will you feel inside me?"

She wanted me to turn her on.

Fucking hell, she would be the end of me.

"Thicker than you can imagine," I said into her hair, fighting hard to stay quiet. The last thing I wanted was either of the other men interrupting us. We'd have to stop, and I'd probably have to kill them.

"And how will I feel?"

"Slick. Tight. Hot."

She continued moving her hand slowly, as if she was taunting me. "How do I make this better for you?"

"Rougher." I growled the word, unable to stop myself.

Her hips arched slightly. "Is that how you'll fuck me? Roughly?"

Her fingers tightened, and I fought back my release as she gave me exactly what I'd wanted.

"If that's how you want to be fucked."

"What if I don't know what I want?"

"Then I'll give you a little of everything, so you can choose."

My body strained as she jerked me harder, and faster.

"You'll be good to me," she said, confidence in her voice.

"Always." I grabbed her hand, stopping her motions as my cock throbbed while I fought my release again. "Wait." My voice was as rough as her touch.

She slipped her free arm beneath my shoulder and dragged her fingertips lightly over the inside of my wing. It was one of the least sensitive spots—but it set me off.

My face twisted into a snarl as I fucked her hand hard. The scent of her desire thickened around me as I coated her fingers with my release, pleasure easing my tension immediately.

My gaze burned into her dilated brown eyes as she held my cock through the final jerks of my climax.

"That was the hottest thing I've ever done," she whispered, making me throb again for her.

Fae didn't have the same limit as human men.

We could release twice before we needed to rest.

And if touching me was the sexiest thing she'd ever done, I'd better step up my fucking game.

After a quick listen to make sure Kyle and Travis were still asleep, I rolled Molly to her back.

She blinked up at me, confused.

She didn't expect me to ensure she had far more pleasure than I did.

The woman hadn't learned yet, but she would. Quickly.

I unbuttoned her shorts and slid her bikini bottoms down her legs. Her breathing picked up as she let me strip her. The cameras would still be rolling, so I didn't dare toss the blanket aside the way I wanted to. Though someone would cut out anything private before putting it on TV, I didn't want the editors seeing a shred of my female's pleasure.

When she was bare from the waist down, her sweater pushed up to her abdomen, I shucked my shorts and tucked her close against me, spooning her from behind.

She sucked in a sharp breath when my erection wedged between her ass cheeks, sticky with the pleasure she'd given me.

"Cam," she whispered, her chest rising and falling quickly.

"Close your eyes. I don't want the cameras to see anything but you sleeping against me," I murmured.

"They'll still hear u—*oh*." The last word was a breath, as I throbbed against her back entrance.

Beneath the blankets, I took her slick hand and guided it between her thighs.

"What are you doing?" Her whisper was hot.

"You're going to play with yourself, with my release." I nipped at her earlobe, tugging lightly on the piercing I loved to play with.

Her hips arched back, pressing my cock tighter to her center. "Am I?"

"Mmhm. Stroke your clit for me."

She moaned softly as she traced a slow circle around the sensitive bud with her slick fingers.

I sucked lightly on her throat.

When she was fae, no mark I gave her would linger for more than a few minutes. We healed quickly.

While she was human, she could wear it for hours, maybe days. And I wanted her to.

I sucked harder on her throat. The intensity made her curse, jerking her hips.

"Now, put my pleasure inside you," I murmured.

"I'd rather put your cock there," she whispered back.

I throbbed hard between her cheeks. "You don't get that until you've chosen me, Lollipop."

"Thought I already had."

I eased her fingers down to her slit and guided them slowly into her channel, pushing them all the way in until her slick palm was pressed against her core.

Her breathing was faster.

The scent of her pleasure even thicker.

"Permanently," I said.

"You think you can handle three more days of this before giving in and filling me?"

"Yes. The first time I'm inside you won't be beneath a blanket, on an uncomfortable wooden pallet. You'll be spread eagle on our bed, watching my thick cock enter you."

Her breathing grew heavier. "You just want me desperate for it."

I chuckled. "No. I just want to hear the sounds of your pleasure when you come with me inside you." I pressed her palm harder against her core, and she couldn't stop herself from grinding against it.

I throbbed against her backside, and she groaned quietly. "You're killing me here."

"It'll be worth it, Loll."

I sucked on her throat again, in the same spot I already had. The spot I wanted to mark her.

"Bastard," she breathed.

"*Clever* bastard." I slid her fingers slowly out of her body, and she made a noise of complaint. "You're going to smell so strongly of me tomorrow, neither of the men will dare flirt with you."

She started to protest, but I slid two of my fingers into her channel, and she cut herself off with a sharp breath in.

"Feel how tight you are for me?" I murmured. "We'll need three days to get you ready for my cock anyway."

I slowly ran my fingers up the inside of her channel, searching for the spot she'd need me to find. The slight roughness took a moment to locate, but when I did, her hips jerked violently. My cock slid against her back entrance as she moved, and she cried out loudly.

I covered her mouth with my palm to cut off the sound, pausing to make sure she hadn't woken up Kyle or Travis.

It brought me intense satisfaction to know that she'd lost control of herself to the point where she physically couldn't keep quiet.

My ears strained as I waited.

There was movement in the shelter closest to us.

Travis.

His snoring had cut off, too.

"Not another sound, Loll," I murmured into her ear, soft enough that he wouldn't hear. "Now you have to wait until he's asleep again."

The expression on her face was one of agony as she tipped her head back to rest against me.

"I know, gorgeous." I sucked on her throat again, my fingers still filling that tight little channel and my cock still stretching those sexy ass cheeks.

Her breath rose and fell quickly, but silently.

It took a few minutes, but Travis eventually fell asleep again.

"Bite me if you need to. Those sounds of pleasure are only for me," I murmured, tightening my hand over her mouth as I finally started fucking her with my fingers again.

Her g-spot was easier to find the second time, and I had her entire body jerking moments later as she finally unraveled. Her cries were quieted enough by my hand that neither of the other men stirred.

Removing my hand from her mouth, I buried my fingers back in the soft strands of her hair but didn't pull my fingers out of her body.

The woman was nowhere near ready for the size of my cock —but I'd tremendously enjoy getting her there.

"You're so fucking sexy," I murmured into her ear, my erection still against her ass.

"How are you still hard?" she panted, trying to stay quiet as she caught her breath. Her channel was still tight around my fingers.

"Fae men can climax twice before we need to rest." I sucked on her throat once more. The mark I was leaving there was getting gloriously darker. "And we recover faster than humans."

"Shit." Her chest was still rising and falling rapidly.

I itched to free her of the sweater so I could have my way with those perfect tits, but it would've required changing our position and removing my fingers from her.

Which wasn't happening.

There would be time to play with her breasts later.

All the time in the world.

"This was supposed to be about you," she said, meeting my gaze.

My lips curved upward. "It is. It's about me watching you climax, repeatedly."

Her face reddened. "*Repeatedly*?"

"Of course. I'm just getting started with you, Lollipop."

I slid my fingers out of her, and her hips rocked, once again sliding my cock against her back entrance. The friction made her suck in a breath. I was slick with both of our releases—and that only made me harder.

"What are you—shit." She cursed softly, hips arching again as I pressed three fingers against her entrance. Her channel was so fucking tight around me, I nearly climaxed at the feel of it.

"You want my cock. This is how you get ready for it," I said, sliding them in further.

Her hips rocked again, desperation in her eyes. "That feels *so* good."

"I'll feel better."

She laughed breathlessly.

I ran my fingertips lightly over her g-spot again, brushing her clit with my thumb, and she detonated.

Her jaw was clenched, her body bucking against mine as she moved. The motions were so violent that our shelter creaked a few times—and she froze as she came down from the climax, realizing the noise she'd made.

Her eyes were wide.

Her channel was tightening again.

I sucked on her neck in the same place to darken my hickey.

The group shelter creaked too, and I heard Kyle mumble something in his sleep.

A moment later, silence descended again.

"We should stop," Molly murmured, catching her breath again.

"Should we?" I removed my hand and added a fourth finger before I started pushing into her again.

Her head tilted back against me. "You're going to kill me."

"No, Lolli. I'm going to make sure you learn what it's like to *live*." I filled her with my fingers and sucked her throat as I worked her clit again, slower but harder.

She squeezed my fingers and cock with her pleasure, crying out against my hand as she lost control once more.

"We have to be done," she moaned softly. "I'm going to be sore tomorrow."

"Good." I started to pull my hand free, to give her time to recover, but she caught my wrist before I could.

Her eyes met mine. "Don't move. I'm not ready for you to move yet."

My lips curved upward. "Good." I kissed her nose, and she couldn't fight her own soft smile.

When she relaxed against me, I relaxed too.

Finally, she was mine.

sixteen

MOLLY

KYLE'S heavy footsteps in the forest woke me up. He always crunched more leaves and sticks in the morning than everyone else combined. I'd be so damn glad to get away from him in a few days.

The sound of him taking a piss close enough that I could hear made me scowl, and I started to roll over.

And then remembered where I was.

And what position I was in.

Shit.

My back was pressed to Cam's front.

His erection was between my ass cheeks, ensuring I was still wet with desire even after sleeping a few solid hours.

One of his hands was tangled in my hair.

The other was buried inside me.

There was an ache in my lower belly that could only be some mixture of desire and soreness. I'd never experienced it before, but I'd never had anything as thick as four of Cameron's fingers inside me.

Definitely not for an entire night.

Kyle was still stomping around, so I had to be quiet if I decided to get up.

But… did I want to get up?

Cam's cock throbbed, and I sucked in a breath.

No, I definitely didn't want to get up.

Not until I'd gotten off again to relieve some of the tension in my middle, at least.

The man behind me was still breathing evenly, telling me he was asleep. He wouldn't have pretended. He had no reason to, and it just wasn't his personality.

He knew he was winning the show, and he had no reason to hide anything from me anymore.

Especially considering how horny I was, and how much fun he apparently had watching me climax.

And given how exhausted he had looked when I found him wide awake in the middle of the night, I was sure he needed the rest.

But… Kyle was still stomping around.

So Cam probably wouldn't stay asleep much longer anyway.

He had been tense, too. A release could help him.

And given the way we'd fallen asleep and everything he'd said to me, it was safe to say he had no qualms about the kinkier side of things.

So, I slipped my fingers between my thighs and teased my clit slowly. The motion made me tighten around his hand.

His fingers curled slightly, the tips brushing the inside of my channel, and I bit back a moan as I continued.

His lips were on my throat again a moment later, sucking lightly. "Good morning, Sunshine," he murmured.

I bit back a snort at his reference to my sweatshirt.

"Woke up a little needy, hmm?" he said, as I rocked lightly against him.

"A little."

He pulled his hand from his hair and used it to remove my fingers from my clit, then rolled me to my back. His cock was no longer against my back entrance, and I ached for the pressure of it,

Then, he slowly slid my feet up toward my ass, opening me up and changing the angle. My head tipped back at the way the sensations changed, my face twisting in pleasure.

His fingers felt amazing—but I wanted more.

"I need your cock," I breathed.

He rumbled. "Not today, Loll."

"*Please.*"

"Beg all you want, Beautiful, but you can't have me until we're off this island."

I groaned softly.

He started to move his fingers, as if he was thrusting in and out, while he toyed with my clit. I was already so turned on, it didn't take long to find my climax.

I came down from the high panting, with my knees open and my bare center only concealed by the blanket. The fabric hid his hands from me, so I couldn't see him touching me—but I wanted to see him.

"Lolli," he warned, as I started lifting the blanket.

"Screw the cameras," I whispered.

My entire body clenched when I saw him.

His hand *owned* my core. Between the fingers buried inside me and the thumb on my clit, it looked like he was gripping me. Holding my pleasure.

And shit, he was doing it perfectly.

"You like watching me touch you?" he asked, sliding his fingers out and back in slowly as he toyed with my clit. "Like seeing your release on my skin?"

"Yes." I breathed the word, and reached for his cock. His shorts were somewhere on the floor of the forest, and neither of us gave a damn.

He was still hidden beneath the blanket too—so I lifted it higher to see him.

Holy hell, what a cock.

Massive and thick, he was already throbbing for me again.

My body clenched tighter.

I wrapped my hand around him, and his eyes closed as his jaw clenched.

"Kyle's awake," he gritted out.

"Don't bring up Kyle while your fingers are inside me."

"We don't have much time until Travis is up too."

"We'll be quick." I started working his cock roughly, and his lips twisted in a snarl.

"That's the last thing I want with you."

"We'll have all the time in the world when we're off the island. For now, don't hold back."

He didn't.

We both came hard and fast, and Cam leaned over my body as he caught his breath.

His expression was still intense, though his shoulders were more relaxed. "That was fucking hot, Loll."

"It was." I wrapped my arms around his neck and used the grip to pull him closer.

He hugged me tightly to his chest. "Only two more days."

For the first time on the island, excitement curled in my middle. "Two more days."

We were so, so close.

And now that there were no secrets, maybe we could even enjoy it.

CAMERON BURNED the mess off our skin before he scooped me up and carried me off to our part of the beach. The sun was still rising, but we'd heard Travis moving around too, so there was no need to be quiet while we washed ourselves off.

He assured me I wouldn't get a UTI despite our less-than-sanitary sex the night before. Apparently, fae magic was good for that too. I wasn't sure it would really help me, considering it was *his* magic, not mine. But, even in the worst case, we were leaving in two days.

Which meant he'd be turning me into a fae in two days.

And any infection I had when I changed would simply vanish, which would be cool.

Cam and I sat on the beach after we washed off, our legs sprawled out in front of us and our sides pressed together. We were on the edge where the water met the sand, and the tide was rising.

"You've never told me much about your family," he said, as a small wave rolled over my calves.

"You haven't told me much about yours," I countered.

He chuckled. "I had to keep my life private to qualify to come here."

"I know. But you haven't told me since then. And I didn't tell you, because it seemed silly to try to bond with someone who showed no interest in my past."

"I wasn't allowed to show interest, but I *am* interested. And my family... well, we're close. It's just my parents and I, though Rhett sort of joined us recently, which I did mention. They went through many rounds of fertility treatments to have me, and have never shown desire to repeat the process for another child. I can't say I blame them. Twenty years of trying and failing, of dealing with that heartbreak and the physical pain my mother had to go through, would be too much for many people. I don't know that I could survive it."

"But they did."

"Yes. And I am eternally grateful for that."

"Are they good parents?"

"The best. They're more like friends now—I'm too old for the relationship to be the same. But I always knew I was loved, and that we were a team. Even now, I can go to them with my fears and feelings."

I smiled sadly. "That sounds really nice."

"It is."

"What are the odds that they'll hate me?"

He snorted. "You'll be saving my life when you become mine, Lolli. They'll love you."

"Saving your life doesn't mean they have to like my personality."

"It doesn't, but they will. You're passionate, you're fun, you're sarcastic... you'll fit right in."

I hoped so.

"My parents were amazing," I said, looking out at the ocean. Another wave rolled over us, reaching my knees that time. "They loved each other, and me, fiercely. They would've had more kids if the world wasn't on the verge of ending when they had me, but they chose not to risk it. I lost them in the war, three years before you guys stepped in and saved the world. He was a doctor, and she was a nurse. They both died saving lives."

Though my eyes were on the ocean, my mind was on the past.

On the people I'd loved and lost.

Tears welled in them, and I didn't try to wipe them away. Sometimes, letting myself feel sad for a bit was the best way to accept the emotions and keep living.

"I was still a teenager, then. Seventeen. I could've joined the fight, and I wanted to, but my grandma guilt-tripped me into staying with her. She thought I needed to grieve, and she was right. I don't think I'd fully moved on when the war ended, and you showed up at her door. Hell, I don't know if I've even moved on *now*."

Cam set his hand on mine. "Grief has no proper timeline, Lolli. It strikes when it decides to, and it stays as long as it chooses."

"Who did you lose?"

"Many friends. We fought our hardest to end the war without exposing ourselves and our magic. We should've stepped in the way we did much sooner."

I nodded. "Some people say the fae won the war, even though it was between humans. Because of the way you took over."

"No one wins a war, Loll. We're just the ones who stopped it." He slipped his hand beneath mine and laced our fingers together. I held on tightly, needing to feel his support more than I realized. "Your grandma will be thrilled when she finds out we've mated."

A sputtered laugh escaped me. "You have no idea. The woman is obsessed with you."

He flashed me a grin. "I bet she watches every episode the moment it comes on."

"I bet she emails the Society daily in an attempt to convince them to let her watch the episodes *before* they come out."

His grin widened. "All of her friends probably watch it with her."

"And they all probably have to fan themselves when Kyle and the other bastards walk around naked."

"They won't be rooting for me, simply because I wear shorts," he said.

We laughed together, and I leaned my side against his. He didn't release my hand, holding firmly even as the laughter faded.

"Do you really think they'll like me?" I finally asked, my voice growing softer. We both knew I was talking about his family.

I wasn't good at making friends. My only friend options were at work, and they all knew that I wasn't going to be there long.

Everyone had been waiting for the Society to call me in for *Bachelorette*. They didn't treat me like one of them. The women acted like I was fae—but one they didn't want to fawn over, considering I had tits.

The men acted like I was invisible, not wanting to accidentally piss off Cam.

"I think they'll like you more than they like *me*," he said.

Another laugh escaped me.

We stayed on the beach for a few hours, talking and letting the water wash over us.

It was blissful.

TWO DAYS PASSED BY SLOWLY, but peacefully.

Travis and Kyle tried to convince me to choose them a handful of times each, but they weren't pushy. I think we all knew they'd already lost.

When the third day came around, we all walked to the voting place for the final time.

Rhett stood beside me while the three guys were instructed to sit down.

"Congratulations to all three of you," Rhett said, studying the group of us. "You are the final survivors. Now, the game rests in Molly's hands. Do you have any questions, Molly?"

He looked at me.

I shook my head. "Nope."

Rhett looked back at the guys. "Now, you all get the chance to say a few words about why you think you should win."

Kyle cleared his throat. "I'll go first."

He stood and took two steps forward, so we were face to face. "Molly," he began. "When we first met, you clearly disliked me."

I winced.

Cam snorted.

"But I used that to get myself to the end of the game, outsmarting everyone except the two men here with me now. I caught fish for you and won nearly every challenge, proving myself to be a damn good protector and provider. What more could you want in a man? Choose me, and you'll live a happy, healthy life." Kyle dipped his head.

Then he captured my hand and lifted it to his lips so he could kiss my knuckles. He did it so quickly that I didn't have a chance to pull away.

Then he winked at me, and took a seat.

Travis was on his feet before Kyle had even sat down all the way.

"I watched everyone from the beginning," Travis said. "I waited until I could see who was controlling the game, and realized it was Kyle and Cameron. Because they were the two you disliked the most, I worked with them, letting them do the dirty work and take the fall for it. No one saw me as a threat, but I was always going to make it to the end, because I allied with the right people. I deserve to win," he said.

I tucked my hands behind my back as he finished speaking, so he wouldn't be tempted to grab me.

Since my hand was out of reach, he set a palm on my shoulder and squeezed lightly.

I tried not to grimace at the unwanted physical contact.

If Cam and I really could change the way *Survival* worked at some point in the future, we needed to make more rules about touching.

When Travis sat down, Cameron finally stood.

His steps were calm but confident as he strode over to me. He took the time to smack both other men on the arms as if in congratulations on his way to me.

His lips curved when our eyes met.

"Hey, Lollipop," he said.

"Hi, Cam."

"I started falling in love with you the day I began guarding you," he said simply. "I kept the secrets I was required to keep, and made sure nothing I did would disqualify me from being here, fighting for you. On the island, I managed to convince every other asshole that I wasn't a threat, blended in with the crowd until I couldn't do that anymore, and fought my way to the end. I did it because I love you—and because I cannot and will not imagine a future without being by your side." He didn't take my hand, or touch my shoulder.

Instead, he went back to his seat, leaving me with that.

I was in a bit of a daze when Rhett gave me a rose—a connection to *Bachelorette*—and told me to choose.

I was still in that daze when I crossed the room and put the flower in Cameron's hand.

And when he pulled me into his arms and kissed me.

Confetti rained down on us, congratulations followed, and champagne was dispersed.

When that was done, we were led to yet another speedboat.

The cameras remained at the island, filming our departure, as the boat carried us away.

And when we were left on the beach of a small island that held a massive mansion, we were finally alone.

seventeen

MOLLY

I STARED at the mansion for a long minute before Cameron pulled me to his chest for a massive, crushing hug.

My arms wrapped around him, and I hugged him back just as tightly. "Is it actually over?"

"It is. No more cameras. No more lies," he said into my hair.

"It doesn't *feel* over."

"It'll take time to adjust to being out of the game, Lolli. Let's go inside."

I nodded against his chest.

Instead of releasing me so we could walk together, Cameron scooped me up off the ground.

A shocked laugh escaped me as my feet popped into the air, my legs hanging over his arm as he carried me princess-style.

"What are you doing?" I asked, unable to fight my smile.

"Carrying you to and over the threshold. Human movies say that's a necessity right after marriage."

"We're not married, Cam."

"No, but we're about to be mated. And that's much more permanent." He winked at me.

I bit my lip in an attempt to stop myself from smiling back.

He carried me up a hill and through a massive set of double doors. I stared up at them—and out into the mansion—with awe as we continued onward.

The place was stunning.

Expensive stone floors.

Elegant tall ceilings.

Gigantic chandeliers

The biggest kitchen I'd ever seen.

A dining room that could probably hold three dozen people.

"Who else is coming here?" I asked him, as he carried me through the place without a glance at any of the things I was staring at.

"No one. There'll be ready-to-cook meals in the fridge, and more than enough groceries to get us by. We're on our own, finally."

My stomach tightened just a little at the words.

I wasn't nervous about the sex. Everything we'd done assured me that would be incredible.

But being permanently mated to anyone was a big change.

Becoming a fae was, too.

What if it hurt?

Or it didn't work right?

Or—

"I can see you worrying, Lollipop" Cam said, his voice playful. "You should know by now that I won't let anything hurt you."

"Except you," I pointed out.

"Those times were by necessity, not choice. I'd never *choose* to hurt you. Not physically, emotionally, or any other way."

I believed him.

"I'm just worried about the change," I admitted. "And the fact that we're sealing our bond permanently. That seems big. And permanent."

I'd said permanent twice.

Oops.

But the permanence *was* a huge deal.

"It is," he agreed.

A moment of silence passed.

My stomach tightened further as we walked past a second dining room that was even larger than the first.

How many dining rooms did one house need?!

"We should fuck on that table," Cam said, as we passed the room.

My eyebrows lifted. "On the *table*? That doesn't sound comfortable."

"No, but it sounds hot."

My brain put together an image of Cam feasting between my thighs while my legs hung off the edges of the table, and I flushed.

Alright, it *did* sound hot.

"Now I want to know what you're picturing," he said, reaching a grand staircase at the end of the dining hall.

"What are you picturing?" I countered.

"You, on your stomach. Bare tits on the wood. Hands pinned behind your back while I fuck you."

My entire body heated. "Shit, that's intense."

"Your turn."

"I was just picturing you going down on me while I sat on the edge."

Cam's chest rumbled in satisfaction. "We'll definitely make that happen."

At the top of the staircase, he walked through an elegant set of double doors and into what looked like an old-fashioned sitting room. There was no TV, just couches and chairs that faced each other. I did notice a mini kitchen to the side of it, though with a fridge that definitely didn't look old-fashioned.

My stomach rumbled at the sight.

"I'll figure out food while you're in the shower," he said.

My eyebrows lifted. "I thought you wanted to seal the bond here and now."

He flashed me a grin. "You're covered in sand, Loll. It's making you miserable. And tense. When I make you mine, you won't be thinking about the sand on your scalp."

I relaxed slightly.

Cam wasn't in a hurry.

He wanted me fed, clean, and comfortable.

"Is the change going to hurt?" I asked him.

"No. It'll be pure pleasure." He set me down on my feet in the bedroom and squeezed my ass lightly. "There's got to be clothes somewhere too. I can look for them after I find us something to eat."

"Thanks."

He wasn't going to make me walk around naked, either.

Things were already much better than they could've been.

He brushed a kiss to my mouth before leaving me in the bathroom. His shorts hit the ground on the way out of the bedroom.

He was just as tired of them as I was of my green bikini.

And *damn*, that was a nice ass.

Closing the bathroom door behind me, I turned the lock and leaned my back against the wood.

The room was silent.

Silence during the day felt alien after being surrounded by noisy strangers for so long. Granted, they weren't strangers by the time the game was over. But still.

I wasn't sure whether to enjoy the quiet or feel weird about it, but the privacy was nice.

The bathroom didn't have any windows, which was even better.

After a moment, I finally stripped my shorts off and untied my swimsuit's double-knots. It took some time, but I got them undone and left the worn, sandy, green fabric on the floor.

It felt bizarre to know no one was watching.

Good bizarre, though.

I slipped into the shower and spent a few minutes scrubbing everything beneath the hot water. I washed my hair three times with the fancy shampoo on the shelf, and let the conditioner sit in it for ages while I exfoliated every part of my body.

I felt lighter when I got out and dried off.

I was *done*.

I survived the game show.

I survived the hunger, the heat, and the island.

I picked a mate I could trust—even if I didn't know everything about him yet—and it was over.

I was never going back.

Relief and gratitude brought tears to my eyes as I leaned against a wall, staring at myself in the large mirror over the vanity.

I wasn't the same person I'd been when I went in. I was different.

Stronger.

Weaker, too.

But different.

And my reflection showed that.

My face was thinner, after surviving on little more than fish for so long. My curves were smaller. My eyes were harder.

The woman in the mirror didn't feel like me, but I had to imagine it would take time to get back to that. Especially if I was about to watch my body change with the bond.

"You okay in there?" Cameron called out, knocking lightly on the bathroom door.

"I'm good." It didn't feel like a lie.

I was fine.

Just... different.

"I found the clothes the Society left and heated up a mountain of chicken fettucine alfredo. I'll leave the clothes outside the door. Alfredo's in the dining room downstairs. I'm going to start eating, so take all the time you need. I'll save plenty for you," he said from behind the door.

The words eased whatever worry I'd had.

Cam was going to give me as much space as I wanted. He wasn't in a rush. He wasn't going to force me to do anything.

He was still Cameron. The Cameron who had guarded me, and the one I knew on the island.

I didn't know how he would change when we became mates, but I didn't think the change would be for the worse. If anything, it should just make him calmer and more confident, because he no longer had to deal with shitty possessiveness and the fact that he was fading.

Right?

I couldn't say for sure, but that was my assumption.

I heard him leave the room, then waited a few more minutes

before I finally let out a long breath and opened the bathroom door.

Sure enough, one of my suitcases was on the floor.

I had packed it with all the others when I was boxing everything up, so someone must've moved some of my clothes.

There was a luggage tag on the top with my name on it, and it didn't look like it had been opened, so I didn't think Cam had snooped.

He could've been the one who packed it, though.

I closed the large bedroom's doors and locked them, then lifted my suitcase onto the bed and opened it up.

Everything inside was folded neatly and separated in fabric packing cubes. On top of them, there was an envelope with my name on it in pretty cursive handwriting.

My forehead creased as I opened the envelope and pulled out the card. Two printed photos fell out with it, but I read the card before bothering to pick up the pictures.

Dear Molly,

Thank you for fighting for my son. I've waited centuries to see him happy, and started believing I'd never get the chance. I haven't seen him smile the way he does with you since he was a wild little boy.

Welcome to the family!

Love,
Christina Cassette

P.S. It's tradition for the compatible mate's mother to fill this bag. I saw that your grandmother packed nothing but racy lingerie, and figured you'd prefer something more comfortable after spending so much time on the island. I put the things she provided in a duffel and had them shipped to Cam's home.

P.P.S. Couples usually only get a week in the house provided by the Society, but I convinced my husband to change it to two for Survival. It'll be a much more difficult transition from the island to mating to reality.

P.P.P.S I had nothing to do with you getting thrown out of an airplane. I was furious for your sake when I found out. Cameron's told me about your fear of heights! And yes, I should've written this letter a few days later so I didn't have to add so many post-scripts. My husband says I'm forgetful, and unfortunately, he isn't wrong.

My lips curved upward at the note.

Cam was right.

His mother already liked me.

And he had told her about my fear of heights, which meant he'd talked to her about me before.

That alone made me warm.

Her casual, friendly letter only added to that. She obviously wasn't too concerned with seeming silly, considering how many additions she'd made to the note. The lettering on each of them got smaller, which amused me more.

And replacing the racy lingerie with something more comfortable?

I could kiss her for it.

Or maybe I could kiss her son for it.

I picked up the pictures, and paused as I looked at them.

Both were of Cameron. The left one was him on the island, sitting next to me on the beach and wearing that familiar grin that lit up his whole face.

The right one must've been before I knew him. His hair and clothes were still the same style, and he was smiling, but that smile didn't reach his eyes.

Christina had wanted me to see the visual difference.

I bit my lip and tucked the photos back into the envelope with the letter. Then, I went through the clothes as I unpacked them into a nearby dresser.

There were two sets of my favorite brand of leggings, as well as two sweaters.

And a variety of bras and underwear in different styles, all of which looked designed for comfort, not sex appeal.

Two sets of sleep clothes, both with tank tops and shorts. One was silk, and one was cotton.

A new black bikini that looked far more supportive and comfortable than the one I'd been stuck in on the island.

A soft night dress with spaghetti straps and lace that was tastefully sexy.

And a silky white robe.

Damn, I liked Cam's mom.

I pulled on a pair of comfortable underwear without touching the bras, then tied the silky robe around my waist.

Padding down the stairs, I managed to find the dining room pretty easily, but stopped when I reached the doorway.

Cam was sitting at the end of the table closest to me, so I was facing his side. His wings and horns were tucked away, his hair was wet from the shower, and all he had on was a pair of soft-looking black joggers.

He looked just like he had before *Survival*, but with a little more sun.

The man was gorgeous.

And he was going to be *mine*.

Despite my original lack of enthusiasm about taking a mate, that knowledge made me feel powerful.

When Cam spoke, people listened.

When he walked, they moved.

When he told them to leave, they did.

Being a fae—and being his mate—would change my life.

And not for the worse.

He was so lost in the pasta that he didn't notice me watching him, which made my lips curve upward.

My gaze moved over the chiseled muscles on his arms, shoulders, and abdomen.

Those were mine, too.

I warmed slightly, and his head immediately jerked to the side. His nostrils flared, and his eyes moved down my body almost predatorily.

The way he looked at me made me shiver in the very best way.

"Hey, Cam." My voice was soft.

"Eat with me, Lollipop."

I padded across the room and slipped into the chair beside his.

He thought it was too far, so he hooked his foot in the leg and pulled it over until the side of it was pressed against his.

Then, he set his hand on my thigh.

The white robe only fell a few inches down my legs, so it didn't conceal much skin. I was pretty sure he'd see my gray cotton panties if I moved. I just didn't care.

The top of it hung open widely, revealing plenty of cleavage but keeping my pointed nipples out of sight.

It made me feel sexy, honestly.

Cam's hooded stare ramped that feeling up.

He loaded his fork for me with the tiniest of glances at the massive casserole dish, then held it out to me.

"You've got to be hungry still," I said, accepting the fork and taking a bite.

"Never said I wasn't."

I tried to hand the fork back, but he only accepted it long enough to reload it and give it to me again.

"Cam," I protested.

"I don't want pasta, Lolli."

My cheeks flushed.

Oh.

"Take the bite," he said.

It wasn't a command, but it felt like one.

And the order felt loaded in a way that made me do it without hesitation.

His chest rumbled. "Keep eating."

My forehead creased when he slid his chair back and stood.

The crease disappeared a moment later, when he lifted me onto the dining table, slid my ass to the edge, and opened my thighs.

My panties were on the floor in a heartbeat.

His mouth found my clit in the next.

My hips arched my body closer to his mouth.

He nipped at my clit.

I gasped.

"Eat, Loll," he growled against my core.

I ignored him, arching harder when he sucked my clit.

"That wasn't a request." He stopped tasting me, his eyes locked with mine from between my thighs.

"I'm not hungry for that either," I breathed.

"I need you fed before I can take this further. Eat."

Though it was the last thing I wanted to do, I finally put a bite of pasta in my mouth.

Cam teased my clit with his tongue, licking and tasting until he gave the command again.

"Eat, Loll."

I groaned, but did.

He gave me what I wanted while I followed his orders—without letting me climax—and when I finally put down the fork, too full and horny to eat anything else, he stood.

MOLLY

CAM DIDN'T PICK me up off the table and carry me straight upstairs like I expected him to.

Instead, he kissed me.

Slowly.

And peeled my robe off when he did, letting the silk fall to the table.

The kiss caught me off-guard, but not in a bad way. Not at all. I hadn't made out with someone in years, and I'd forgotten how much I liked it.

The kiss was hot, and my need swelled with every minute that passed.

My legs hooked around Cam's waist, and I rubbed myself against him as he kissed me, needing the friction to push me closer to the edge.

Right before I managed to climax, he pulled my legs off his hips and lifted me off the table by my ass.

I groaned into his mouth, and he trailed his lips down my throat as he carried me up the stairs.

"You don't get to come until you're wrapped around my cock, Lollipop. We're done playing games."

We reached the bedroom quickly, and he set me on the edge of the mattress before stepping back. I thought he planned on taking his pants off, but instead, he just looked at me.

Slowly.

Hotly.

"Fuck, I am a lucky man," he said, running a hand over his stubbly chin. "Open your thighs for me."

I opened them, leaning back on the bed as my legs hung off.

"Wider, Lolli."

I did as he'd commanded, the need so intense I couldn't help but tease my clit a little.

He growled low in his throat and pushed his joggers down his thighs. His cock sprang free, thick, hard, and leaking from the tip. "Don't even think about getting yourself off."

"Then give me what I need," I shot back.

"What do you need?" he stepped up to the edge of the bed, just as naked as I was. When he leaned over me, I slowly lowered my back to the bed until our bare chests were touching.

"You." I wrapped my hand around his length, and he growled again for me.

"This is what you want?" He put his hand over mine and guided his cock to my core, dragging the head of it over my clit.

My hips jerked, and I released him. "Hell yes."

The words earned me a low, sexy chuckle. "Alright, Lollipop. You remember the words?"

The words...

The vow.

The mate bond.

I nodded, and he lined us up.

Then, slowly, he thrust in.

My thoughts went blank.

Any and all words died way before they reached my throat.

The tip of him was inside me—stretching me—and he was huge.

The feeling was unreal.

"Breathe," he ordered, and I took a shallow breath.

Cam opened me wider, and sank in another inch.

My chest started rising and falling quickly.

The fullness...

The intensity...

"Are you sure you're going to fit?" I groaned.

He chuckled roughly. "I'm sure, Loll. How are you feeling?"

"Good. Full." I managed.

"You feel fucking perfect. Better than perfect. Do you need a minute?"

"No."

He thrust lightly again, and I gasped as he filled even more of me.

"Keep breathing." He stroked the inside of my thigh lightly.

"Is it always going to feel like this?" I moaned.

Because it was good—but overwhelming.

So overwhelming.

"Tight, yes. But not this tight. Your body will adjust for me during the change."

He thrust in another inch.

My back arched, but he held me in place.

"You're doing perfect, Loll."

I moved my hips a little, taking him in deeper.

He gritted his teeth.

"Give me all of it. I don't want to wait," I ordered, though still breathless.

"It'll be better if—"

"Now, Cam." If he got to give me orders, he could follow mine too.

He growled, but thrust.

A cry of pleasure tore through me as my body arched, tightening around and against his thick erection. He'd bottomed out inside me—and he wasn't going anywhere.

I was so, so close to the edge—but I couldn't finish.

Not until I bound us together, like he wanted.

Needed.

And I needed that too.

"I'm yours," I said. "I'm yours, Cam."

He growled fiercely. "And I'm yours, Lollipop. Forever."

He thrusted hard, and I detonated.

My scream of pleasure tore through the air as my body moved with the intensity of the climax.

Cameron snarled with his release, and the heat of it dragged out my orgasm even longer.

My back arched.

My body rocked.

Warmth rolled through my veins.

And I felt my shoulders sort of... stretch.

He flipped us so he was beneath me, but I barely noticed the motion.

A new, comforting weight pressed against my upper back as I leaned over him, panting and holding myself up with my hands on his chest.

His were on my waist, his grip firm enough that I knew he'd catch me if I started to crash down.

"I have wings, don't I?" I whispered, still struggling to breathe.

"You do." His eyes held mine, his fingers not reaching for the soft feathers I could feel brushing my bare back.

"How do they look?"

"Almost as stunning as the rest of you." One of his hands lifted to my breasts, and he dragged a finger lightly over my tight nipple. I rocked a little, and his lips curved upward. "How do they feel?"

"Weird. Heavy."

He chuckled. "It'll take time to adjust to them."

"I'm sure. At least I won't have horns. My head would get too heavy to hold up."

He snorted. "You'd manage."

"I don't think so." I tried to raise my wings, but nothing happened when I did. "I don't think I can move them."

"The muscles will strengthen over the next few days. How much can you feel them?"

"I don't know. Touch one."

His eyes heated. "If I do that, you'll have to ride my cock again, Lollipop."

"Last I checked, I *am* still riding you."

His lips curved in a wicked smile. "Must've forgotten."

"Liar. You're still throbbing inside me." I moved my hips, and his wickedness faded, replaced with pure lust.

His fingers lifted to one of my wings, and I shuddered violently as he lightly touched the center of it.

"Sensitive. Too sensitive," I choked out. "Not in a sexy way."

"Sorry, Loll." He captured my nipple again and pinched it lightly. "You feel amazing. Let me make you feel good again."

"Are you *asking* if you can fuck me while you're still inside me? That's counterintuitive. Just do it."

Those wings were really damn heavy.

My gaze was locked on his hand as fire danced over his fingertips.

Where his fire touched me, pleasure sizzled against my skin in a deliciously foreign way.

He trailed his fingers down my abdomen until they reached my clit, and holy hell, the intensity of his magic had me arching and climaxing with just the smallest touch.

The hand he didn't have on my center remained on my hip, holding me up through my pleasure.

When I collapsed against his chest, trapping his arm between us, I was panting again. My heart beat wildly, and I tried desperately to catch my breath.

"What are you doing to me?" My body was trembling, and I somehow still wanted more. The thick erection still buried inside me wasn't doing anything to ease that.

"Making you mine, Lollipop." He captured my mouth with his, and I couldn't help but kiss him back passionately. His fire reignited, and he carefully rolled us over again. I sucked in a breath when my wings met the blankets, but the light pressure felt nice after the initial shock.

When he started to move again, it was slower.

Sweeter.

More intimate.

And as we found our releases together once more, it didn't feel like fucking.

It felt like... something bigger.

Maybe even a little bit like love.

CAM LIFTED me back on top of his body after we came down from the high. His cock was finally softening beneath my hip, and I was more relaxed than I'd been in ages.

Maybe ever.

He had one of his hands buried in my hair again, and was teasing the damp strands lightly as he played with them.

"Well?" he asked me.

"Well what?" I mumbled against his chest.

"Well, do you hate me again?" His voice was playful, but I heard something in his words. Something almost hesitant.

"I never hated you, Cam. If I did, I would've picked Kyle."

He snorted. "It would've been a terrible choice, really."

I laughed. "He's not that bad when you get to know him." After a pause, I amended the statement. "For some people. Probably."

"Maybe."

I couldn't fight my smile. "Your mom left me a note in the suitcase. Did you read it?"

"No. I assumed your grandma packed it."

"She did, first. Apparently it was full of racy lingerie."

Cam laughed. "That woman really does love me."

"She does. Thankfully, your mom pulled out everything my grandma packed and replaced it with actual clothes."

"Damn her," he murmured. "I told you she'll prefer you over me when this is said and done."

There was no heat behind the words. Only warmth.

I bit my lower lip, not sure if I should leave it at that or ask him about the pictures.

My desire for knowledge won out after a moment, and I lifted myself up over him again. My hands were on his chest once more, propping me up. "She put two pictures in the letter."

His forehead creased. "Pictures of what?"

"You. Before you met me, and after. She said you're happier with me."

The creases vanished. "Ah."

"Yeah."

He wrapped a strand of my hair around his fingers slowly before admitting, "I wasn't in a great place, mentally, when the conversation I told you about happened."

"The conversation where they threatened to force you into *Bachelorette* and you countered with becoming my guard?"

"That's the one." He continued twisting the strands, then untwisted them before finally going on. "I was in a dark place. Had been, for a while. More than a century."

"How old are you?"

"A few years under three hundred. That's about the cutoff, as far as living without a mate goes. No one makes it to three centuries alone."

Shit.

I knew fae aged differently than humans, but still.

That was a lot of years.

A lot of *dark* years, if what he was saying was true.

"I was hoping my time would be up sooner rather than later. I'd started fading a little. I suppose humans would call it depression, but for fae, it's something even more intense. We begin losing our magic, and with it, our lives."

His gaze was on the strands of hair he was still playing with, wrapping and unwrapping them from his fingers.

"You don't have to tell me, if it's uncomfortable to talk about," I said.

"You deserve to know." His words were simple.

Soft.

Sweet.

My chest ached for him anyway.

"I didn't particularly want a mate. Never really had. I'm sure I could've found one earlier, but the desire wasn't there. I knew it would kill my parents to see me fade entirely, but I wasn't going on Bachelorette. Someone would've died if I had. Possibly many someones. Myself included. Though I countered with the guard plan, I didn't truly *want* it to work out."

Staying quiet, I gave him time to work through his thoughts and feelings.

"But then I saw you," he said, lifting his gaze to mine.

There was something in it.

Something deep, and intense.

"In the introduction video you sent with your bloodwork, you were uncomfortable. Most of the compatible mates were, but you weren't as bad as most. And the sweater you had on—a sweater, despite it being the middle of summer—was yellow."

My throat swelled as I realized where he was going with that.

Why he'd picked me.

His lips curved slightly.

"The words made me snort. *Good morning, Sunshine?* And the skull in the sun? It was fun. I thought, a woman who would wear a sweater in the summer, and hit the Society in the face with sarcasm in the process, was a woman who might be able to pull me out of the dark place I'd been in. So I picked you, I showed up at your door, and found you with that lollipop in your mouth—and you were even more annoyed to see me than I expected. It was perfect."

I bit my lip.

He *had* been quieter when we first met. He'd teased me less.

The longer we'd known each other, the more playful he grew.

And the more freely I teased him back.

"The darkness around me dissipated every day. I don't know if you dispelled it, or if I forced myself to do that because I wanted more time with you, but it did fade. It felt like I was coming back to life. You became my purpose. The center of my world. My everything."

The man had clawed his way back to life because of me.

For me.

It was no wonder he'd voted Chris out.

"And now, you're my mate." He pulled my face down to his and kissed me slowly.

Tenderly.

"What if I'm not enough to keep you here?" I asked, quietly.

"Mated fae don't fade. The magic prevents it. When they pass on, it's either from a wound they can't recover from, or a clear choice they both agree to make."

The slight tension in my shoulders eased.

"You saved me, Lolli. The rest of our lives, I'll do whatever it takes to make sure you're blissfully happy."

"Don't give me credit for that. I just existed. You saved yourself." I lowered my chest back to his and rested the side of my face against him. "This probably isn't the right time to say it, but I think I'm falling in love with you."

"Finally."

I batted his arm lightly, and he laughed.

He'd already said he loved me, so it wasn't like he hadn't reciprocated.

Then, his stomach rumbled beneath me.

"I knew you didn't eat enough pasta," I grumbled.

"Wasn't hungry for it." He sucked lightly on my shoulder, making me shiver. "It won't be long until the mate bond is pushing us together again. I need to feed you before we get there."

I sighed dramatically, but agreed.

My wings still felt heavy as he scooped me out of the bed and carried me back down the stairs—but the weight of them was kind of nice.

MOLLY

A FEW DAYS passed in a blur of sex and food.

My missing curves would surely be back soon. And Cam would undoubtedly appreciate them.

Though the need the bond made me feel was intense, it also left us with plenty of time to talk.

And tease each other.

And laugh together.

Whatever darkness Cameron had been dealing with was clearly long-gone. It made me feel good to know I'd played a part in that, even though I hadn't realized it at the time.

My wings grew stronger every day, and by the time a week had passed, I could finally carry them the way normal fae did, without letting them sag.

Working on our large breakfast of pancakes, bacon, eggs, and way too many hashbrowns, Cam studied me.

I narrowed my eyes at him. "You're looking at me weird."

"I'm doing no such thing." He took an emphatic bite of his bacon and didn't look away.

"You definitely are."

He took another bite.

"Spill the beans, Cam," I warned.

His lips curved upward. "Alright. I'm thinking it's time to test out those wings."

My eyes narrowed further. "Absolutely not. Have you forgotten my fear of heights? And the way Rhett literally *threw* me out of a plane?"

"Just think about it. If you learn how to fly, there's nothing to fear from heights."

"Like hell there isn't."

"I'm serious, Loll."

"So am I," I shot back. "Drop it. I'm not doing it."

He sighed, but agreed. "What should we do today, then?"

The sexual need was fading a lot, which meant we were going to have free time.

A lot of free time.

I considered it.

We'd already caught up on sleep, and made up for all the missed meals on the island. We'd hashed out the unknowns and issues between us, so there was none of that left.

"We could go to the beach," he suggested, his smirk telling me he already knew how I felt about that.

I snorted. "If we're tossing out ridiculous ideas, we could build a blanket fort and watch romcoms all day, too."

He considered it like it wasn't ridiculous.

"You're not actually thinking about a blanket fort, right?" I checked.

"I am, actually." He took another bite of bacon. "And I'm liking this idea a lot. You never invited me to watch movies with you in our apartment."

"You never asked if you could watch with me."

"I wasn't allowed."

Right.

"Do you seriously want to have a romcom marathon?" I asked.

"I think I do."

Hot damn.

That was kind of sexy.

He finished off his bacon and lifted a finger at me. "Don't go getting turned on before I get the chance to put this blanket fort together. It will be the perfect sex cave."

I laughed. "You're insane."

"You love it." He winked at me, and I couldn't fight my grin.

I kind of did.

ONE BLANKET FORT, a few rounds of sex, six chick flicks, and a few hours of sleep later, we were back at the table for another breakfast.

"I know what you're going to say," Cam began. "But I really think we should get you flying while we're still on the island. You don't want to adjust to being a fae without flying. It could make learning really difficult in the future."

"Not happening." I bit into my waffle viciously. "I have absolutely no desire."

"But—"

"Isn't there a pool somewhere in here? I've smelled chlorine a few times."

Cam gave me a warning look. "You're changing the subject."

"Your mom put a new bikini in the bag. I could try it out." I leaned over the table. "Or we could go skinny dipping."

His eyes heated. "We need to practice flying."

Despite his words, I could tell I was about to win the argument.

"The only time I've been skinny dipping was with a guy in high school," I said.

As expected, a possessive gleam flashed in Cam's eyes. "Where? When?"

"There was a lake outside the town. I was a junior."

The water was so cold that we only went in to our ankles. I'd only been naked in front of the guy for a total of three seconds before I yanked my clothes on and got back in the car.

But Cameron didn't need to know that.

Yet.

I'd tell him after he was thoroughly distracted by swimming.

"If we're skinny-dipping in the pool, I want you naked on the beach afterward," he finally said.

I made a face. "You know how I feel about sand."

"You know how I feel about flight practice."

"Pool and sand sex it is."

Cam didn't let me finish my breakfast before he hauled me down a hallway I'd never been through, and to a large indoor pool.

THE NEXT MORNING, I was running low on ideas, so I suggested hiking.

He didn't love the idea, but I talked him into it once again.

We spent the day walking around the island, checking out absolutely everything. He knew I was just trying to avoid learning how to fly, but he held my hand and chatted with me the whole time anyway.

It was surprisingly fun.

When we got back, we showered and crashed in bed, watching another movie before we fell asleep together.

THE NEXT DAY, he brought his idea to the breakfast table.

"I want you to fly with me."

I scowled.

Before I could shoot him down, he rephrased it. "You haven't seen my phoenix form yet. I want you to fly on my back. We can look down at the *Survival* island while we do, to see if the next season has started filming yet."

My unhappiness vanished. "Do you think they have?"

"Probably. There are so many fading fae, they don't have time to wait. I'd imagine they're a week in by now."

Damn, I hadn't thought about that.

I sat back in my chair, grimacing.

"You could bring the new girl a set of your clothes if you think it would help her."

"That's a good plan. I thought shifting would exhaust you, though."

And I still didn't want to deal with the heights thing.

"It will," he agreed. "When we get back, I'll need to sleep a lot for two or three days. Which will buy you more time to avoid learning how to fly."

I perked right up at that. "I'll pack a bag for her. Then, we'll go."

We finished our breakfast before heading upstairs together. I gathered a few things while Cam searched for his care package backpack. It was hard to decide what to pack, knowing how important every little thing was on the island, but I finally settled on a blanket, a pair of leggings, and a sweatshirt. I grabbed my toothbrush and hairbrush, too. Though she'd probably rather have fresh, clean ones, anything was better than nothing. I would've even shared a toothbrush with *Kyle* on the island if it meant having clean teeth.

"Are you sure the Society isn't going to have an issue with this?" I asked, as I accepted the backpack he handed over.

"Nah. Seeing us again will probably increase the human views, which mean the show will continue happening. They need it to keep running, considering how many of us can't handle *Bachelorette*. As long as we don't say or do anything to affect the game's outcome, it'll be fine."

I nodded.

We could keep things neutral and still make the next girl's time a little easier.

I unzipped the backpack, and stared down into it when I saw the little box at the bottom.

Shit.

I'd forgotten about that.

I pulled it out slowly, lifting it up to show Cam. "What was going through your mind when you packed this?"

He gave me a soft smile. "I want to claim you in every way there is, Lollipop. Even the human way."

My face warmed.

Though I was coming around to the idea that we were mates, accepting that we were married felt different. Probably because I hadn't been raised knowing fae existed, but I'd always believed in marriage. Seeing how much my parents loved each other ensued that.

I tucked the backpack beneath my arm and opened the box.

Inside, I found the most beautiful ring I'd ever seen. There was a tastefully-large diamond in the center, with a unique halo around it that made me think of a picture frame.

"It's beautiful, Cam." I lifted my gaze to him. "Are you sure? Marriage seems like a pretty big step. I don't think most fae wear wedding rings, and—"

He plucked the box from my hand. "I'm sure, Lolli." Pulling the ring from its resting place, he got down on one knee in front of me. When my eyes widened, he winked. "We're already more connected than any pair of humans can be, but will you marry me?"

I bit my lip.

"Your grandma will want to watch you say I do," he added.

"Alright, you win." I held my hand out to him. "I will."

He put the ring on my finger, then pulled me into his arms and kissed the hell out of me for a good solid minute.

I kissed him back just as passionately, until he pulled away.

"Now, I believe we were about to take a detour so you can avoid learning how to fly?"

"Yep!" I stuffed the things I'd gathered into the bag. Cam had to help me wrestle them down so I could get it to zip, but he did so without me asking. "Let's get going."

WATCHING HIM SHIFT WAS INCREDIBLE. I couldn't hide my awe as he shifted from a gorgeous man to an elegant, gigantic bird. The gold on his feathers covered his entire body.

When I ran a hand down his side, he preened for me, making me laugh.

It took a minute to figure out how to get on his back, but I eventually managed. And when I did, I didn't hesitate to lean against him.

My stomach clenched as he tensed, ready to take off, and it rushed into my throat as Cam took to the sky.

I clutched his feathers for dear life, squeezing my eyes shut as I fought off nausea. My own wings tilted naturally in response to the wind against them, but I didn't pay them any attention.

Thankfully, I managed to keep from throwing up as Cameron leveled out in the sky. He flew much more smoothly than I expected, and after my nausea faded, I opened my eyes slowly.

We were gliding over the ocean, with tiny islands beneath us as we went. Though it scared me at first, I eventually calmed down enough to appreciate the view.

The wind rustled my hair and wings, feeling surprisingly nice against my feathers.

We didn't have to fly for long. It must've only been twenty minutes later when we approached a beach I recognized too well, and saw a few familiar guys waving at us lazily.

Kyle's shock of blonde hair caught my attention right away, and I found him grinning like usual.

And naked.

Cameron landed on the beach, but didn't shift back. The guys there congratulated us, a few of them slapping him on the back and laughing about how he outplayed them.

I figured shifting back would be the beginning of the exhaustion he mentioned.

I noticed Rhett sitting on the edge of the sand, glassy wings sprawled behind him and a permanent scowl on his face.

Maybe Cam's parents really *had* made him play. The new girl was nowhere in sight, so he couldn't have been guarding her.

When the guys greeted me, they were nothing but polite. And the leggings and t-shirt I had on made me feel much more comfortable around them than the tiny bikini ever had.

Cam and I made our way over to Rhett after the greetings.

"So, who's the new girl? And where is she?" I asked Rhett, scratching Cam's feathers to say goodbye to him for a few minutes. We wouldn't stay long, not wanting to mess with the game and risk pissing off anyone.

"Erin," he said, giving exactly zero other information.

Hmm.

"I brought her a few things to make the island more comfortable," I said. "I'll go look for her."

He nodded in the direction he thought she was, and I gave Cam one last pat before I headed off that way.

The soft sand between my toes felt much more homey than I expected.

I greeted the guys I knew in passing and waved at the one I didn't recognize. They directed me down the beach as well, so I kept moving.

When I found Erin, she was already headed to me. Her skin was pale, her wavy, naturally red hair tied up in a ponytail on top of her head. She was built strong with killer curves, and dressed in nothing but a black sports bra and a pair of what looked like running shorts in the same color.

She raised her eyebrows when she saw me. "How the hell did they talk you into coming back here?"

I laughed. "They didn't. I packed a few things to make your trip a little more comfortable. Any way to stick it to the Society for dropping us here."

Her lips curved upward a little. "I can appreciate that. Thank you. Nice wings, by the way." She gestured to the golden appendages I had a love-hate relationship with. "How is it, being a fae?"

I shrugged. "Could be worse."

She snorted. "Could it, though?"

I said a quick goodbye before going back to Cameron. He took off from the beach, and I hollered a good luck to everyone as we flew away.

My curiosity was so strong, I didn't have time to think about the fact that we were in the sky again.

And while my stomach still clenched a little at the distance between us and the ocean below, I felt better about it.

A lot better.

· · ·

I SPENT the whole trip back trying to figure out what her plan must've been—if she had one—and when we landed, asked Cam what he thought immediately.

He shifted back, and though his expression was tired, he grinned at me in a way that said he knew something I didn't.

"What are you hiding?" I asked.

"What will you give me for an answer?" he teased.

I stepped up to him and put my hands on his chest. "How about a blowjob?"

His eyes flashed with heat. "Deal."

The bastard would've told me anyway, but I'd been wanting to see how he reacted to having my mouth on his cock for days.

He carried me through the front doors, and I made love to him with my mouth just inside the mansion.

When he told me what he'd heard from Rhett afterward, I couldn't help but laugh.

twenty

MOLLY

WE SPENT a few lazy days watching movies and napping while Cam recovered from shifting. He didn't bug me about flying, and I didn't bring it up either.

The morning of the last day of our private island honeymoon, I poured two glasses of orange juice. Then, I sat out on the balcony of our room and watched the sunrise. My feet were propped up on the fancy metal railing, and the sun's rays felt amazing on my skin.

Cameron was in the shower, and I was completely and utterly relaxed despite the uncomfortable chair I occupied.

A light breeze blew past, ruffling my hair and the feathers on my wings. I closed my eyes, relishing the feel of it.

Some part of me had been itching to fly again ever since I rode on Cam's back. Something about having the wind against my skin sounded amazing.

But flying would mean accepting that I'd changed. A lot.

And I wasn't sure I was ready for that.

So I sipped my juice and enjoyed the feel of the wind.

I heard the shower turn off and opened my eyes so I could watch the waves crash lightly on our private beach again. Despite my hatred of sand, spending a month and a half living on an island had made the beach feel like home.

"We'll have to take trips to the ocean sometimes," I told Cam, as he sat down in the chair beside mine and grabbed the glass of juice I'd poured for him. We were just about out of food, but there was still juice.

"Think you'll miss it?" There was amusement in his voice.

"I wish I could say no, but I think I will," I admitted. "Or I'll miss the sound of the ocean, at least. I love that."

He nodded. "It's calming."

"It is."

"Which is why my main home is on the beach. Remember the pictures I showed you? Maybe I should go looking for that asset folder again." The tease in his voice was soft.

"Oh, right." I bit my lip. "I haven't pictured what our life will be like. Didn't think about the beach house."

"There have been a lot of changes in a short period of time. Adjusting won't happen overnight."

Another breeze blew past, and my wings lifted slightly of their own volition.

"You want to fly, don't you?" His voice was soft, but playful.

"Maybe." I freed my lip from between my teeth. "I don't know if I'm ready to leave and accept all of this, though. This is... a lot." My gaze went to the glittering ring on my finger, and lingered there. "We're mated, permanently. I still haven't wrapped my mind around that. Add in the wings and the magic, and I feel like I'm in over my head."

His hand landed on my thigh. "Change is always difficult."

"Even for a gorgeous, ancient fae?"

He feigned offense. "I'm hardly ancient."

I snorted.

He chuckled, squeezing my thigh. "No one ever gets used to change. We just learn to accept it as inevitable."

Nodding my head, I watched a few more waves crash. "Part of me is afraid."

"Afraid of what?" His thumb started lightly tracing shapes on my leg.

Some of the guys I'd been on the island with would've taken my fear as a personal attack, so I appreciated tremendously that Cam didn't.

"I'm not really sure. The other humans, maybe. I know I'm not getting a job again, since we'll be working with your parents, but I worry about interacting with them. They treated me differently even before I had wings."

"That's their fault, Lolli. Not yours. Insecure people will find reasons to hate you no matter what you do or don't do."

I nodded again. "Yeah. I just don't want to deal with it, I guess. I kind of miss being human, before I was a compatible mate. I was normal, back then. I didn't think to appreciate it."

"Luckily for you, you are now an extremely normal fae woman."

I flashed him an amused look, slightly surprised.

"Less than ten percent of female fae were born that way. That makes you part of the majority. No one you meet in our world who has magic will find you anything but entirely average."

A laugh escaped me.

Warmth flooded my chest. "You know, that actually does make me feel a little better."

"Good." He leaned over and grabbed my waist, lifting me off my chair and setting me on his lap. Part of my wings pressed lightly to his chest, but the contact felt nice. "The only thing that would make you abnormal is refusing to fly."

I snorted. "Of course it comes back to that."

"Just doing my job." He pressed a kiss to the arch of my wing, and I shivered.

It was a good shiver, that time.

Maybe the uncomfortable sensitivity was finally in my past.

"Let me teach you how to fly, Loll. You'll love it," he murmured, kissing the shell of my ear next.

I let out a long breath. "Alright, fine."

He kissed my cheek, then stood up and set me on my feet. "It's easy. You'll love it."

He towed me out to the beach, and we spent the next few hours in the sky.

Cam was right.

It was easy.

And I did love it... almost as much as I loved him.

twenty-one

CAMERON

AFTER WE LEFT THE ISLAND, we spent a few days at my parents' place. They did in fact love my mate even more than they loved me. Molly and my mother were partners in crime before the first day ended, which told me I should dread the coming years.

I didn't, though.

I looked forward to them, as much as that would've surprised my past self.

After three days at her grandmother's house—who was *my* new partner in crime—and a small, intimate outdoor wedding, we made our way home.

The apartment we had shared was already occupied by another compatible mate, but that wasn't home.

Home was wherever Molly was.

The Society had moved her things to a home I owned near my parents' favorite house. It wasn't a secret that we'd be taking over for them after the next vote, which would take place in six months. We had six months to learn everything we needed to—and Molly was surprisingly excited about it.

I chalked that up to her being pissed about the way she'd been thrown out of that plane.

I opened the beach house's double doors for Molly, making sure there was space for her wings before she stepped through. She kept bumping them into things, and they were so sensitive that it hurt badly. So, that had become my task.

I enjoyed it tremendously.

Particularly because it gave me the chance to brush my fingers over them frequently, which always made her shiver.

I hadn't had the chance to play with them the way I wanted to yet, but we had time.

All the time in the world.

Molly looked around the furnished home, nodding her head as she checked it out. She wasn't one who enjoyed decorating, but I knew what she liked, and I'd made sure it would satisfy her long before we moved there.

"It's beautiful," she admitted, walking out onto the balcony after the tour was over. "And look, it comes with sand."

I grinned, tucking an arm around her waist and plopping a kiss on her forehead. "Your favorite."

It wasn't where I wanted my mouth, after a week of stolen moments and quiet sex in other people's homes, but I'd still take it.

"It would be a shame to separate me from it," she agreed.

"The biggest of shames."

Turning, she wrapped her arms around me. "You're a good man, Cam. I'm glad you fought for me on the island."

"Careful, or you'll make me hard with your compliments," I murmured into her hair, earning another soft laugh.

"Who said I didn't want you hard?"

"The uncertainty on your face told me plenty, Lollipop."

Her humor faded.

"I'm not uncertain. I want you. I love you. I'm just still adjusting. I'm excited for the future, but I still don't even feel like this new body is *mine*, you know?"

I made a noise of agreement. "I think I can help with that?"

"Really? How?" The hope in her eyes was enough to make me pause and kiss her, tangling my fingers in the long strands of hair I enjoyed teasing so much.

She kissed me back without protest as I walked her backward, until we were in the nearest bathroom. I had to block her wings from hitting the doorway twice, but the scent of her desire grew thicker in response both times.

Inside, I finally released her mouth and turned her around slowly, protecting her wings once more.

"What are you doing?" The curiosity in her gaze was almost as sexy as the swell of her lips, red from my attention.

"Showing you how perfect you are. Stand still."

I peeled her sunshine sweater, altered to fit her wings, down her arms and to the ground.

Her soft, gray bra followed.

I gave myself a moment to play with her breasts before sliding her shorts and panties down her thighs, exposing her whole, beautiful body to me.

She was stronger than she had been before the change.

Her curves were more pronounced, though that was mainly because of how much I'd been feeding her. I'd always loved cooking for her, but after watching her starve on the island, I loved making sure she was getting enough to eat.

And framing her stunning body, were the golden wings that marked her as fae.

And as mine.

"Look at this gorgeous, smooth skin," I murmured into her ear, slowly trailing my hand up her soft, bare abdomen.

Her face reddened, just slightly.

The scent of her desire was impossible to ignore.

"These perfect breasts." I finally let myself take the handfuls I wanted, and ran my thumbs over her tight nipples. She rocked her ass lightly against my erection, and set her hands on the bathroom countertop to steady herself.

"I'm going to touch you now, Lollipop," I said against her ear.

She took an unsteady breath in.

"When you watch yourself climax, I need you to remember one thing."

"Okay," she whispered, gripping the counter tightly. "What?"

"That I love you, you love me, and we're going to figure out everything, together. For the rest of our eternity."

She nodded, her eyes shining with emotion.

And as I touched her body, bringing her to orgasm, I reminded her over and over that I loved her.

That she loved me, too.

And that we were going to be a team, forever.

epilogue

MOLLY

BY THE TIME Cam finally let me out of the bathroom, I was so well-pleasured that my legs were shaking.

And as silly as I'd thought his plan was at first, it actually kind of worked.

My body felt more like mine.

I guess it helped that the house he owned honestly felt like home.

Or maybe it was just *him* that felt like my home, so the location didn't matter.

"Are you ready for this?" I asked, folding myself onto the gigantic, comfortable couch that took up way more space than it should've in the living room.

I absolutely loved it, though.

I had on Cam's favorite sweater, and a pair of comfortable volleyball shorts that had never seen any kind of sports game in their entire life.

They had seen plenty of couch time, though.

"Ready to watch Rhett kick some ass," Cam said, pulling me onto his lap without hesitation.

I smiled as I turned on the first episode of the second season of *Survival*. It technically wasn't available to the public yet, since our season hadn't even finished streaming, but all of Cam's connections came in handy sometimes.

"I don't know. I'm kind of rooting for Kyle," I said, barely holding back my snort.

Cameron laughed so loudly, it caught me off guard and I almost fell off the couch.

Which made me laugh.

Which made him laugh, again.

Fuck, life was good.

"In his dreams," Cam said, setting me on the floor at his feet. Before I could complain, he was massaging my shoulders, and I was relaxing completely.

He tickled my side, and another laugh escaped me before he resumed the massage.

We watched closely as someone else's future played out in front of us.

Survival of the Mated had been hell... but it gave me Cameron.

And that made everything worth it.

afterthoughts

Oh my gosh.
OH MY GOSH.
I had SO MUCH FUN WITH THIS BOOK.
So stinking much fun.
Hopefully you did too. Even if you didn't, I'm just gonna
pretend for the sake of this afterthought, okay?
I've had this idea in my head for probably nine months now.
So, compared to the expansive collection of other ideas, it
really hasn't been around all that long.
But I couldn't get it out of my head.
I just couldn't.
And somehow, it was just as much fun as I expected.
That never happens.
NEVER.
But here I am, nine writing days later, with a complete story
that I am head-over-heels in love with.
Sometimes, I love this job.
Most of the time.

Err, fine, I'm a bad liar. It's sometimes.

But this time?

This time I love it.

So, yeah.

That's where I'm at.

I've always been a big *Survivor* fan, so oh my gosh, I'm about ready to write a hundred of these books.

Which I won't do. Because boredom will set in.

But hey, I'm having fun, so let's not say never!

If you liked this one, you are going to LOVE Erin's story.

She's pissed about being on the island, and ready to stir up some chaos.

And so is her love interest ;)

Her book will be called Glamour & Gumballs. The main title on the cover will be Survival of the Mated, but anyway, check it out!

As always, thank you so much for reading!

Until next time!

<3 Lola Glass

stay in touch

If you want to receive Lola's newsletter for new releases (no spam!) use this link:

LINK

Or find her on:
FACEBOOK
TIKTOK
INSTAGRAM
PINTEREST
GOODREADS

all series by lola glass

Standalones:
Survival of the Mated
Mate Mountain
Wildwood
Deceit & Devotion
Claimed by the Wolf
Forbidden Mates
Wild Hunt
Kings of Disaster
Night's Curse
Outcast Pack
Feral Pack
Mate Hunt

Series:
Burning Kingdom
Sacrificed to the Fae King
Shifter Queen
Wolfsbane
Shifter City
Supernatural Underworld
Moon of the Monsters
Rejected Mate Refuge

about the author

Lola is a book-lover with a *slight* romance obsession and
a passion for love—real love. Not the flowers-and-
chocolates kind of love, but the kind where two people build
a relationship strong enough to last. That's the kind of
relationship she loves to read about, and the kind she tries
to portray in her books.

Even though they're fun stories about sassy women and
huge, growly magical men ;)